BEACH SUNSET

BEACH HOUSE ROMANCE
BOOK 4

JULIE CAROBINI

Beach Sunset (Beach House Romance, Book 4)

JULIE CAROBINI writes inspirational beach romances from her home on the California coast. Please visit her at JulieCarobini.com.

ONCE UPON A TIME ...

I wrote a series about five siblings who inherited a beach house—with a catch!

That was in 2020 ... and we all know what happened *that* year. Life was turbulent so I decided to do something different: I released all five books under a pen name.

But ... I found it difficult to maintain two personas. I also wanted to add a bit more content to these stories. So I pulled the novels from publication, added new scenes, and re-covered the series under my own name.

If you like tropes, such as fake relationships, billionaires, secret babies, and cowboys, then I know you'll love the revised and refreshed Beach House Romance series!

Now, turn the page for book four ...

Julie

1

Lacy almost let the call go to voicemail. She glanced out to sea, the brim of her hat shading her skin from the sun's afternoon glow, the lounge chair comfortable against her back. Her time at the family beach house had come, just as it had for three of her siblings who had already put their month of labor into the place. But with all the excitement surrounding Maggie and Luke's sudden re-coupling and the impending wedding-of-the-year for Jake and Daisy, no one seemed to notice that she had arrived.

Well, except for her boss, Adrian, who kept barking orders from the next state over. The man was likable enough, but rather wimpy, too—he whined a bit much for her taste. Poor guy had a weak heart, she was told. So she tempered her bite whenever she responded to his outlandish requests. No sense in aggravating the man's precarious medical condition.

Still, he threw so many requests her way:

Could she make a few calls on prospective clients while out there?

Do a secret site inspection in Santa Barbara?

Snoop around when the President's motorcade arrives in Los Angeles and find out what dessert they're serving at lunch?

The immediate answers that came to her mind were maybe, probably not, and no.

But all she actually said was, "I'll look into it."

Her cell phone rang again, the name "Wren" splashing across the screen. Lacy took a long sip of her sangria, gave the sea another glance, and answered the phone.

"Oh! You are there, dear."

Lacy sighed. "Hello, Wren. How may I help you?"

"I'm in a bind," the elderly woman said, her voice nearly frantic. "I do hope that you'll help me."

Lacy frowned. Wren Mcafee had been one of her mother's closest friends in this beachside town. She'd had a stroke, but survived it, thanks to Lacy's sister and husband, who swooped in and saved the poor woman. Now she was on the mend and living right next door like she always had. Pretty soon, her daughter, Daisy, would be marrying Lacy's brother, Jake. And just like that, they would all be related.

"I will certainly try."

"Wonderful. It's a rather delicate matter and I'm hoping, well, I am pleading with you to keep a secret. You will, dear, won't you?"

A tickle of a smile found Lacy's mouth. What kind of secret could a near-invalid have? "Scout's honor."

Wren hesitated. "Were you ever in scouting?"

"For about a day and a half."

Wren chuckled. "You sound like my Daisy. Of course, I would have asked for her help if she was home. But since you are the daughter of one of my dearest friends, God rest her soul, I just knew you'd help me."

Lacy held her wineglass lazily, swirling the liquid in the glass, her mind wandering back. She vaguely recalled the pie Wren would bake and bring over soon after her family would roll into Colibri Beach for their summer stay, and that her mother would pull a knife out of the drawer to slice it up. There was coffee, too. Always so much coffee. She could almost smell it.

Lacy ran her tongue over her top lip. "What is it that I can do for you, Wren?"

"Oh! You see, the Sullivans next door to you rent out their house and I try to keep an eye on things for them."

"The Sullivans?"

"You remember them, don't you? Young couple with hoards of money who own the house on the other side of your family's? Well, they are quite a bit older now. Off living in New York, I believe. Or is it Long Island?" She released a breathy little sigh along with laughter. "I suppose it really doesn't matter, now, does it?"

Lacy nodded her head as if the motion would somehow encourage Wren to wrap this up. She had some serious navel-gazing to do.

"Anyhoo, the Sullivans now use their spare home as a vacation rental and, boy howdy, do people complain about that. That's the secret, dear, by the way."

"That the house is being used as a short-term rental?" What did she care? For all intents and purposes, she was on vacation too. Except for that bothersome little detail regarding her parents' will and her obligation to fulfill her part in all of that.

Wren broke into her thoughts. "Yes. The Colibri Coastal Association is all in a titter about short-term rentals. Says they're for addicts and partygoers."

"And yet there's no law against it, correct?"

"That is true."

"So if there's no law preventing STRs, then there is no way to prevent anyone—the Sullivans, you, me—from renting out our property should we like to do so. Right?"

"So does this mean you will help me?"

Lacy shrugged, though there was no one around to see it. "Sure."

"Well then, what I need you to do is run the key over to the vacationers when they get here. I also have a map of the area you can give them."

"A paper map?"

"Now don't you try to tell me they'll use their smartphones." Wren tsked. "I want these people to feel welcomed in Colibri, not as if they have to muddle around and try to find things on their own."

Tension began to creep up Lacy's neck. The sooner she ended this call, the quicker she could get back to, well, doing absolutely nothing. Just the thought of an unencumbered moment was ... divine.

"Yes, Wren. I will take care of that for you. I will be over shortly to pick up the key."

"Wonderful! Please meet Mr. Johnson at the property at five p.m. I so appreciate this, dear."

Lacy swirled the wine in her glass, thinking. How many times had Wren called her "dear"? She frowned, tilting her head. "Wren, before we hang up, I need to ask you something ... do you know who I am?"

"Why, yes. You are one of the Holloway sisters."

"Hm. Which one?"

"Um, let me see."

Lacy stuck her tongue into her inner cheek, her frown increasing. "My hair is long and dark and rather straight," she said. "I used to carry around my camera and take photos of sea life in the mornings. Do you remember now?"

"Ah, yes. I do. You're ... you're the one in the middle!"

Lacy downed the last of her drink. She shut her eyes, released a sigh, and disconnected the call.

THE FIRST TIME Finn noticed Lacy she was standing in a trade show booth debating a sommelier about the finer points of Syrah, a red wine that she called both assertive and elegant. It was not lost on him that the banner over her booth advertised a hotel with the word "budget" in its name.

She was better than that.

He moved closer, intending to surreptitiously pick up her business card from the draped table and be on his way. As he did, she broke free from the rather cross wine connoisseur's stare down, flashed him a sociable smile, and offered him her hand.

"Lacy Holloway."

"Finn Hastings."

Her smile, though firmly professional, grew warmer. "A pleasure. How may I help you?"

In those few minutes of conversation, Finn learned all he

needed to know. She was experienced and under-employed, flexible, and savvy. As CEO of Hastings Resorts, Finn knew she would be perfect to take the reins from his brother, Adrian, when he was ready to let them go. For Adrian's health, Finn hoped that would be sometime soon. Very soon.

The following week, Finn handed Adrian, who ran his flagship resort property in Las Vegas, Lacy's card and said, "Hire her."

Finn glanced out the tinted window of the Escalade that sped north along the coast, the driver occasionally pointing out spots of interest along the way. "Lots of evening surfers out tonight, sir," he said at one point. And later, "If you are feeling hungry, I could drive you to a restaurant for a bite."

Finn flicked a glance at his watch, anxious to settle in for the night. He'd eaten on the plane, though it was against his usual judgment. At the moment, his gut sank like a boulder. "No, thank you, Robert."

He released a sigh. The flight had been uneventful enough, but long, giving him too much time to think. In the end, he was left with a mountain of "what if" scenarios.

When he had met Lacy, what if ...

He had not recently been through a brutal breakup?

His mind had not been clouded with doubt and uncertainty?

He had seen her as a woman, one who wore her Porsche red dress like it had been crafted for her and not just the next person to run his Vegas resort?

What if ... he had not given his little brother time to fall for her so that he could pursue her first?

Finn closed his eyes, the sun still bold, though it was nearly evening. He tried to shut out the cacophony of road sounds punctuated by the occasional musical note coming from the driver's radio. He could have told him to cut the sound, but why bother? He was only half aware of it anyway, his mind too ensconced in work and past errors in judgment.

"We should be arriving in Colibri Beach soon, Mr. Hastings. Shall I call ahead?"

"Call ahead?"

"To your concierge."

Finn scowled. He was headed into a question mark, an area that by the looks of it on a map was a mix of Mayberry and fog. How had his brother learned about this blip of a place and what made him think it would be perfect for a resort like one of his? He preferred the anomaly of sprawling land in an urban setting. Give city people a place to come and unwind in their own backyard. A place that gives tourists an oasis in the middle of madness. He glanced out the window again. This town looked like a different kind of madness all together: boredom.

"Sir?"

Finn startled. "One moment." He scrolled through his phone looking for information on where he would be staying. He frowned. Only an address and a note that someone would meet him with a key. No contact name at all. Finn sighed. He would have to talk to his new assistant, Helene, about this in the future. "No need to call ahead."

"Yes, sir."

The slip-up from Helene and his failure to notice it until now was the tip of a mountain of issues that needed dealing with, but who could blame him? Six months ago, he'd had the ring and the plan. He would propose to Paige on the anniversary of when they had met: New Year's Eve. He had assembled the same friends and associates who had been there that night. Would she notice? Or would her dazzling eyes be on him alone, as his would be on her, so that all other sights were invisible?

A sarcastic groan left him.

He never had a chance to find out. Instead, he had walked in on them in the middle of the day, as if he had landed the part of a hapless supporting actor in a two-bit movie of the week. He had given her the key to his penthouse because it was closer to the restaurant than her own place. He thought she might like to change her dress after work and splash on some perfume. He wouldn't have demanded it—she always looked refreshing and beautiful to him. But he knew her. Or thought he did. So he had made the offer.

He had forgotten his briefcase that morning, preoccupied by the events of the night ahead. He could have sent his valet back for it. Why hadn't he? He still remembered the shock of finding Paige with ... Brad. Even more than that, oddly, he remembered how he had been smiling idly as he unlocked the door of his apartment and stepped inside, as if he were dwelling on a secret that only he was privy to. That stupid, slaphappy smile. Was that the image she still recalled at the moment their relationship died?

Finn had learned a huge lesson that day. He had not become a billionaire by ignoring his due diligence! And from now on, that would apply to his love life, if he were to ever pursue one again. Until then, he would use this time to focus on what mattered most: his corporation and its future. This next few weeks, though he still was not sure what could come of it, would be a welcome respite from the usual mania of his life. He hoped that it would do him some good.

LACY GLANCED AT THE CLOCK, her face twisting into a grimace. It was nearly five. She had picked up the key—and the map Wren had insisted on including—and now she waited. Annoyed. Though she had chosen sales as a career, the draw of introversion had been strong since the moment she landed on the weathered old porch of her parents' beach house. She had been reluctant to come home as if she was being forced into fighting for her sliver of an inheritance. But now that she was here? She owned it, as in, she suddenly began to wish that she could curl up in a blanket on that old ratty couch and contemplate her life for days.

Her cell rang and she groaned. Adrian again. "Yes?"

Her boss grunted. "You sound bored. I'm glad to hear it."

She rolled her eyes. "Not bored, just ... busy."

"Staging? You're busy staging an old beach house." His laughter was coarse, loud. "You're so talented you could do that in your sleep."

Lacy stiffened. She wasn't used to bantering with the boss, her need for professionalism rising. She glanced around at the house's old decor, the lumpiness of the couch, and that ancient map above the scarred-up dining table. Maybe the old homestead was causing her to lose her edge.

"I apologize, Adrian. What can I do for you?"

"No apology necessary, but I'm glad you asked what you can do for me."

She clamped down on her back teeth, waiting.

"I'd like you to scout your hometown for a new resort."

Lacy laughed.

"Why the laughter? I'm serious."

"Um, I don't need to scout, I can already tell you that this town doesn't fit the Hastings Resorts aesthetic."

"Do it anyway."

She scowled. "Why?"

Adrian grunted. "Because my big brother is breathing down on me like a hot-aired dragon trying to find new sites, that's why."

How rich. Lacy's grimace grew deeper. Didn't Finn Hastings know that Adrian had a heart condition? That he didn't need his big brother to constantly stress him out with orders to undertake impossible tasks? She seriously needed to end her obsession once and for all with ... Finn. So what if he was hot ... smoldering, actually. And that every time they were in the same room together, which sadly, wasn't often enough, she'd had to will herself not to tremble or stare like that first time they'd met.

Thankfully, when she had met him at the trade show, she'd had the presence of mind to treat him with the same respect and professionalism she had everyone else. Doing so had become her habit, something she fell into naturally. Keeping her cool had also kept Lacy from melting into a fan girl right there in that trade show booth. She needled her lip as she thought back to that day, a flush of embarrassment catching her by surprise. Good thing she was alone right now.

Lacy forced herself to exhale. "I'm sorry to hear that, Adrian. Sure. I'll take a look around and see what kind of properties are available here, if that would help you."

"It would. Immensely." She could almost hear the smile in his voice.

If only he would finally take early retirement—due to his medical condition—so she could move into his Director of Sales and Marketing position, as she had been promised. That would be something they could both smile about.

After the call ended, Lacy thought more about Finn Hastings and his unreasonable requests. No wonder Adrian had been bothering her so much lately with a to-do list of his own. Must be difficult to be the brother of a billionaire.

She wrinkled her nose. Technically, she had a billionaire for a brother too—a good guy by all accounts—but who knew how that might change if she were to work for him?

The roll of tires onto gravel caught her attention. She snapped a look at the clock. Five after five o'clock. Duty called. Lacy found the key and the map, put on her sandals, and slipped out of the door and around to the other side of the house.

A black Escalade sat in the driveway next door and she wasn't surprised. The house had been added onto and remodeled, unlike many of the other homes surrounding it, including her family's. The outside looked more like a Spanish villa than a beach home, with white smooth stucco siding, a gabled turret, and a tile roof.

A man in a dark suit stepped onto the porch. Middle-aged with a full head of grey hair, he stood poised to knock on the front door.

"Excuse me," she said, once she had reached the bottom step. "Mr. Johnson?"

The man turned around, his gaze registering confusion.

Or perhaps it was surprise. Whatever it was, he recovered quickly and flashed her a smile.

"Yes," he said. "The house will be for Mr. Johnson. I would like to enter the home and make sure it is suitable for my client before he enters."

Lacy frowned and hesitated. Wren had made it sound like a couple or a family would be renting the place, not some solitary client with a driver. Of course, as she had also said, the owners had hoards of money. Maybe this was one of their friends? Or clients?

As she debated whether to hand over the key or to ask for some sort of identification, she heard a car door unlatch and open.

"Lacy Holloway?"

She froze, the familiar deep voice etched in her memory, though she didn't care to admit that to anyone. Lacy swallowed her shock and turned. "Mr. Hastings?"

"Finn." His eyes, dark as the sport coat he wore, caught with hers. On approach, he reached out his hand to shake hers. "I didn't realize you would be meeting me here."

She accepted his hand, wordlessly.

Finn lifted a look at the man standing by on the porch. "Frank, it appears that Ms. Holloway has already inspected the property, so that won't be necessary."

Lacy snapped out of her trance. "I believe there's been a misunderstanding. I am currently on a sabbatical and staying in my family's home over there." She pointed toward the house next door. "My neighbor, Wren Mcafee, was unable to meet you here, so she asked me to give the key to Mr., uh, Johnson."

Finn smiled. "That's the pseudonym my assistant chose for me this time."

"Hmm."

He quirked a smile at her, a lock of his hair drifting onto his forehead. She resisted the urge to gently brush it back into place. "I take it you don't like the name she chose," he said. "What would you have preferred?"

She smiled, despite the racing of her heart. "I have no opinion."

"I sincerely doubt that. From what I've witnessed, you have plenty of opinions."

He ... noticed? Lacy stuffed down the momentary thrill. He was playing with her and she knew better than to fall apart over it. This was the reason the man was rich, for heaven's sake. Because he knew what to say and when to say it— and he also knew exactly how to make people think what he wanted them to think.

This was one reason her mind was such a scrambled mess at the moment, something she did not like one bit. Only the weak fell apart.

Lacy held the key out to him, ostensibly changing the subject. "Well, I won't keep you. Nor will I ask for your identification, Mr. ... Johnson."

He grinned. "A necessary inconvenience."

"Of course." She kept her gaze steady, professional. "Here is the key to the house, and here"—she handed him the faded paper drawing Wren had entrusted her with—"is a map of the area. Wren insisted I see that you received this."

Finn accepted the key but raised an eyebrow at the map. "I take it Wren is a senior citizen."

"She is."

He licked his lips and took the map as well. Frank swooped down and took them both from Finn's hands. The older man glanced at Lacy. "I will handle things from here on out." He didn't add: *You can go now*. But she heard his meaning anyway.

She turned to leave and stopped. "By the way," she said, "the local coastal group frowns on vacation rentals around here. So you might want to keep your arrangement quiet, you know, so you don't draw any ire while you're here."

Frank nodded. "We'll keep that in mind."

Finn cut in. "Yes, thank you for your insight. I may call on you for more of that."

Lacy narrowed her eyes. The rest of her month was planned out. Well, her plans were at least penciled in and they did not include work for Hastings Resorts. Not that she would mention that right now. He probably was used to getting what he wanted—what was she thinking? *Of course*, he was used to getting what he wanted.

Instead of inserting her thoughts, which could very well drip with unwelcome sarcasm, Lacy pressed her lips together and nodded. "Perhaps we'll talk again." She crossed the divide between their two houses, achingly aware of how her forced vacation had begun a steady downhill turn. Lacy hoped it wouldn't pick up speed anytime soon.

2

————

He was her kryptonite. Why hadn't she realized this before? It was morning now and Lacy stood with one hand on her hip and the other on her phone, surveying the living room and the couch that had clearly held more than its share of teenaged rear ends. She had moved it twice already and was beginning to sweat. But she was determined to figure out the optimal spot right now so she held up her phone camera and took another photo of her current furniture placement. Anything to keep her mind off of the boy next door.

"Knock-knock!" The screen door swung open and Maggie trounced in.

"Someone's chipper," Lacy said, without looking at her sister.

"And someone here is not!" Maggie hooked an arm around Lacy's neck and smacked a noisy kiss on her cheek.

Lacy sighed and looked up at the ceiling. Suddenly her

dreary job in Lost Wages, Nevada was looking shinier and shinier.

Maggie plopped down on the couch and curled her feet up underneath her.

"Really, Mags? I'm trying to find the perfect spot for this thing."

"I'm surprised I didn't find it out on the curb."

"So you agree we should get rid of it."

Maggie scoffed, laughing. "I said no such thing. Although, if you really think we'll have a hard time selling this place without proper furniture to stage it, then I'm sure we could rent one."

"Or have Jake buy us a new one."

"Ha—no way am I asking him. Especially not with that fancy wedding he and Daisy are planning!"

Lacy crinkled her nose. She took another photo, this one with her sister on the old couch. "Why are you here again?"

"Because I can't get enough of my middle sister."

"Stop."

Maggie grinned. "Fine. I stopped by because, well, I want you to come to my wedding."

Lacy stared at her big sister. "You're kidding. I thought you were going to elope?"

"We are. Sort of." Maggie stood up. "Luke and I picked up our marriage license and we've decided to get married a week from Saturday, right here in Colibri."

Lacy stuck a fist into her side. "How is that eloping? Eloping means sneaking off in the middle of the night to get married in some uber-secret place without a lot of hoopla."

Maggie gave her an embarrassed smile. "Don't you think Luke and I have carried enough secrets for a lifetime?"

Lacy sighed. "For sure."

"As to your comment about where we should elope, I want you to know there'll be no hoopla here. We're getting married on Luke's deck and I would love for you to be there. That's it."

"Well, of course, I'll be there, but won't the rest of the family be peeved that you haven't asked them? You were pretty upset with Grace when you learned about her marriage in the news."

"Fake marriage."

"None of us knew that at the time."

"True." Maggie was smiling. Really smiling. "Look. The rest of the clan will be in California soon for Daisy and Jake's wedding. We can all celebrate together then. Luke and I just really, really want to get married. Now."

Lacy shook her head at her beaming sister and waved a dismissive hand in the air. "Yeah, sure, whatever. I'll attend your elopement with a bottle of champagne and a big smile on my face. Happy?"

"Yes!" Maggie rushed her, pulling Lacy into a bear hug like only her big sister could accomplish. "I'm so glad you're here."

"That makes one of us."

Maggie's eyes washed over her face. "You're teasing me, I know. But ..."

"But?"

"Something happened. I can tell. What's up?"

Lacy laughed for the first time in days. "You will never stop being the big sister, will you? I'm fine."

Maggie stared at her quietly, a motherly gaze resting on

Lacy. It unnerved her. Finally, she said, "If you're sure, then, I will go."

"I'm sure."

As Maggie turned to leave, Finn, aka Mister Tall-Dark-and-Handsome, appeared in the doorway. Lacy almost called out *Grand Central Station!* at yet another unannounced guest. Her father used to answer the phone that way when their home was overrun with visitors running in and out.

Maggie spun around, her lips popped open, her eyes equally expressive. She mouthed the word: Hottie! but Lacy shooed her toward the door anyway.

"Hello, Finn," Lacy said as she opened the door. "I would like you to meet my sister, Maggie. Maggie, this is Finn Hastings."

Finn reached out his hand. "It's a pleasure to meet you, Maggie."

"And you as well," she said, casting a questioning look at her sister.

Lacy didn't bite, though. Finn, too, caught eyes with her. "I hope I'm not intruding."

Maggie butted back in. "Not at all. I was just leaving." She turned so that only Lacy could see the hubba-hubba expression on her face as she sang out, "Ta-ta!"

"Come in," Lacy said, holding the door open wide. She'd have to explain his presence to Maggie later, but in the meantime, she wondered what he was doing here looking like he was about to hike the foothills. Though she had always appreciated his taste in suits, the number of times they had bumped into each other over the past couple of years could be counted on one hand. This was the first time she had seen him in anything so ... informal. Hiking boots, shorts, a T-shirt that highlighted the arms and abs of a guy who took care of himself.

"Lacy?"

She snapped a look at him. Had she been staring? Worse, had he noticed?

He smiled. "Is this where you grew up?"

"Yes and no. We spent our summers here." She didn't feel the need to expand on that explanation, though there was so much more.

"It looks well-loved."

A laugh escaped her. "It needs some remodeling, you mean."

He turned and let out a whistle, steady and smooth, his eyes on the kitchen. "Wow. Didn't expect to see that."

Lacy smiled. "Now you're being truthful. The kitchen was a gift from my brother who stayed here a couple of months ago. He's got a great eye, not to mention the skills to carry his vision through." She swept an arm to point out the rest of the house. "Other than some new additions to the guest bath and painting, the rest of the house has remained pretty much unchanged."

He took a step toward the kitchen but paused. "May I?"

She shrugged and almost immediately wished she had been more accommodating. He was her boss's boss, which technically made him her boss. She still found it odd and a little unnerving that he was here in Colibri Beach, of all places. Especially since she had as recently as yesterday tried to shake away all thoughts of him. The way he treated his brother? Please!

Yet now that he was here, she couldn't run off and

pretend she didn't notice him, because, being honest, she couldn't *not* notice him.

Finn strolled through the kitchen, stopping occasionally to admire the lines of the cabinets, the elegant faucet, and the high-end appliances and their shiny finishes. When he had toured the small space, he turned and leaned onto the quartz-topped island.

"There's a lot of wow in this room. I don't suppose I could fly your brother out to New York to update the kitchen in my apartment?"

"Yes, there is a lot of wow in there, and it's doubtful that my brother could fit you in."

Finn's smile faded. "I see."

She wanted to roll her eyes at the look he flashed her, the expression of a little boy who had just learned Santa Claus wasn't real. Instead, she flashed him a bridge-making smile. "Jake is getting married in a few months. Not only that, he runs an architecture firm in Los Angeles and barely has extra time anyway. The kitchen was a side gig, of sorts."

Finn's dark brows dipped as he stared at her. Adrian always called this his formulating face. "When he looks like that," Adrian had whispered to her once, "he's formulating a question or point of view. Best to stay quiet until he's finished."

Lacy licked her lips and waited, decidedly uncomfortable.

Finn's expression relaxed, a certain light in his eyes. "Is your brother Jake Holloway?"

"He is."

He grinned. "I don't know why I never made the connection, nor why you never mentioned him to me."

"Me?"

"He does design hotels, doesn't he?"

Lacy froze. If they were playing chess, Finn had just declared a checkmate and she was about to be thrown out of the game. But in her defense, Jake designed a lot of beautiful things—not just hotels. "Yes, you're right. He does."

Finn's expression sobered. "Small world. Your brother has certainly been on my radar."

"May I ask ... are you looking into building more hotels?"

"The prospect is always alive, though I am very selective."

"That's true. You are."

As if an afterthought, Finn took a quick look at his watch. He glanced up, his forehead creased. "In fact, I have a call soon with a Realtor."

Goosebumps rose on her arm, and not in a good way. "Not with Lillian Madsen, I hope."

His face gave nothing away. "You know her?"

She scoffed. "Everybody knows Lillian. She's a shark."

"Well, this is the beach ..."

"A land shark."

"I see."

Why did he say that so often? "Listen," she said. "I can appreciate the woman's success. She practically owns the listings in this town. That's admirable."

"But?"

"She has a terrible bedside manner."

"I don't understand. Or maybe I do ..."

Lacy shook her head and crossed her arms. She didn't care to talk about this, to bring up the sad things of life, but Lillian had stepped on too many hearts—including her own.

"If Lillian makes you a promise, say, to sell your house, she'll do everything in her strength to get it done. No matter whose grave she has to walk on to make that happen."

He winced. "You really don't like her very much."

"I do not."

"I consider myself warned."

"May I ask why you're speaking with Lillian? Because if you're thinking of buying a second place here in Colibri, I could ask around and see who might be selling."

"Actually, I'm surprised you haven't heard why I'm here."

"Heard?"

"Adrian suggested I look into this area for possible resort development. I thought he would have told you."

Lacy shut her eyes. Of course. In a strange and disjointed sort of way, this all made sense now. "You know, Adrian asked me to scout around for a possible location, and I immediately tried to shut down the thought."

"Why?"

She gave him an exasperated sigh. "For one thing, there's no city or airport near here for miles. For another, there's not a lot of open land left. And on a personal note, my memories of this place are quite mixed."

"I see."

She bit back a retort.

"Did I say something to offend you?"

Remember who he is, Lacy. Don't be curt. "Not at all." She shook her head, trying to convince herself. "I just have a lot on my mind today."

He dropped a gentle fist to the island countertop. "Right. I'll be going now."

"Wait," Lacy said. "I forgot to ask why you stopped by. Was there something you wanted to ask me?"

"I was going to ask you what you thought of my Realtor and you offered me your answer before I had the chance to mention her. I will be on my guard."

"Okay, then."

Finn's eyes took a quick sweep of the living room before returning to her face. "Have a good day, Lacy."

"Mm-hm. You too." She closed the door behind him and leaned her back against it, her eyes landing idly on a thin shaft of light struggling to make its way through a curtained window. Already it had been an eventful day. Finn Hastings had just been in her home, alone, with her. If she had wanted to, she might have steered their time together in a far different direction than it had gone.

Something wriggled in her brain. Hadn't Adrian said that his brother was breathing down on him about finding property to develop? And now Finn was here, searching?

Lacy exhaled, forcing her shoulders to relax. Poor Adrian was obviously being pressured by Finn to find the next great American resort destination. Didn't Finn know the precarious state of his younger brother? How could he justify pressuring him like that?

Lacy knew that she would likely bump into Finn around Colibri Beach. How could she not? But she determined to keep her head—and her heart—in check. The last thing she wanted to do was fall for a man who was so driven to succeed that he worked his flesh-and-blood brother to an early grave.

～

EMOTION HAD no place in business. Finn had learned this early on, the advice steering him toward the mega-success that he had become. Regardless, a surge of something—happiness, perhaps?—washed over him with each crest of a wave. He had been standing at the water's edge for longer than he ever had in his life, watching the rise and fall of those waves, the plunge of pelicans, and the flyover of caustic gulls. The entire spectacle had caught him by surprise. How long had it been since he had walked on the beach for the simple enjoyment of it?

Years. That's how long.

He crossed his arms, his bare feet sinking farther into wet sand. For the first time in many months, Finn let emails wait. He hadn't done so since, well, since Paige. In retrospect, their relationship had merely been a blip in an unending string of workdays, projects, and deals. He'd allowed himself time with her to cause a break in all of that, at least somewhat, because frankly, Paige hated his career. Disliked the travel it involved or hearing about his day-to-day dealings.

So he'd kept them from her, for the most part. Revelations had poured over him in recent months, reminders of things that he had overlooked, such as the way her lip would curl slightly when he would introduce her to a colleague. He doubted they would catch it, as he did, but it was there. Or the way she would release a heavy, yet quiet, sigh when he would ask her opinion about a potential resort site. "Whatever you want, darling," she would say, and get back to reading her iPad.

Unfortunately, he had been too far gone with her, too much in love to notice how she would shut off when he would ask her opinion or share a moment from his day. He should have known better than to allow her to meet a playboy like Brad. A grunt flew out of him and into the wind. Brad's father had written a song that had been re-released ninety-four times in as many ways so he spent his days doing ... nothing. Whatever those two talked about, he had no idea. Maybe they didn't talk at all ...

Finn's phone rang. He inhaled deeply, thankful for the interruption from a drift of darkness over his momentarily happy thoughts. "Finn Hastings."

"So formal, brother."

Finn let his eyelids drop shut briefly. "Good morning, Adrian."

"I sure hope you're not working nonstop out there. You're at the beach, man. Act like it!"

Finn chuckled. "As a matter of fact, I am standing on the sand as we speak."

"Hopefully not in a suit, unless it's a wetsuit."

"Not planning to surf anytime soon, but for your information, I'm wearing shorts."

"Stop it."

Finn laughed outright now. "Stop what. I own shorts and T-shirts. Plenty of 'em."

"Well, well, that I'd like to see." Adrian laughed. "Listen, I don't want you to stop enjoying your vacay on my account, but I did want to let you know that I'm putting in a call later to Lacy Holloway. I'm not sure if you are aware, but she is staying in Colibri Beach at the moment and knows the area very well. I believe she grew up there."

"I'm listening."

"I would like Lacy to give you the grand tour of the area."

Finn bit down on his lower lip. He needed to keep his

head on straight if he was going to determine the right spot for development here—if there was a right spot. Having Lacy as his guide, though, could muddle his judgment. He had figured that out last night when it had taken all his strength to turn around and walk out of her house.

There was a bigger concern: Adrian. His brother kept his love life to himself. Always had. But Finn had noticed the way Adrian's voice seemed to change whenever he talked about the brown-eyed beauty who was his lead sales manager. His gut told him Adrian harbored feelings for her, and the thought caused his own heart to clench—with disappointment.

Even if he wanted to see where things could lead with Lacy, if she were even interested in him, he could not do so knowing that his brother was interested. Especially with his questionable medical condition drawing a question mark over his future.

And not after his own best friend broke his heart by seducing his ... Paige. No. He wouldn't do it.

"Finn? You still there or did I lose you to some beach bunny?"

Finn scoffed lightly. "Here. Listen, I don't need Lacy to show me around. I'm a big boy, little brother."

"I know that."

"I have an appointment with a Realtor out here." He hesitated, wondering if he should mention what Lacy told him.

"The one who told you about some beachfront homes out there?"

"You remembered."

"Of course. She said she knew of a string of homes that

you could buy and tear down to put up the resort. Any thoughts of how difficult it would be to get the zoning laws changed out there?"

"Not yet. I'll be speaking to Ms. Madsen about that, though ..."

"What's wrong?"

He huffed a quick sigh and crossed an arm across his chest and tucked his hand beneath his armpit. "I need to tell you something, Adrian."

"Sounds cryptic."

"It's not really. It turns out that Ms. Holloway is staying in the house next to the one I'm renting."

Adrian paused before replying. "Really?"

"Yes. I spoke with her briefly last night—I was going to mention it to you today—and she warned me that Ms. Madsen's character is less than stellar."

"That settles it then. All the more reason for Lacy to be the one to show you around."

"Maybe."

"What do you mean maybe? Lacy knows the area better than anyone, and her character isn't questionable, so I will speak to her today and set something up."

Finn frowned. The last thing he wanted to do was discourage his brother. He couldn't tell him the truth—that Lacy's presence stirred up an array of thoughts that surprised him, lifted his heart and mind out of the depths. No. He would not go there. He could not hurt his brother like that.

Finn decided he needed to double down on his protests, for both of their sakes. "I consider myself forewarned about Ms. Madsen; however, I don't plan to cancel our appointment. On the contrary, I will meet with her and hear what she has to say and make my decision from there."

"She sounds like a tough one."

Finn chuckled. "You doubt me?"

Adrian sighed. "All right. If you must. When is that appointment? Today?"

"Actually, it's tomorrow morning. First thing." Finn flipped a glance toward the house he was renting, suddenly aware of the ever-growing list of emails and phone calls waiting to be returned. "I will be heading back to the place where I am staying now and working from there for the rest of the day."

"Hogwash."

Finn jerked his chin up and laughed toward the expansive sky. "What in the world does that mean?"

"Same thing it meant when Mom used to say it. You're in Colibri to scout a spot. Lacy's the perfect one to show you around, so don't waste that talent. I'll set something up for this afternoon." Adrian's voice faded as if he turned away from the phone to deal with an interruption. He returned to the call. "Gotta go, brother. Lacy will contact you soon if I have anything to say about it."

The phone went dead, leaving Finn to stand barefoot in pooling sea water and wonder how he was going to keep his emotions ... in check.

3

———————

What part of *I am on sabbatical* did this man not understand?

Adrian's whiny voice flowed through Lacy's phone speaker. "Finn is available this afternoon, so can you do it? Show him around the town? The vacant areas?"

Lacy tossed an empty box into a recycle bin and wiped the back of her hand across her forehead. Even from here she could hear the roar of waves, yet they offered her no comfort right now. She pressed her lips together, thinking. Truthfully, she had barely left the house since arriving in Colibri. Why would she when the town had a food delivery service and the house itself had a front-row view of the ocean?

Adrian's voice broke through her thoughts. "I think I missed your answer."

She rolled her eyes, one hand stuck deeply into her waist. She could refuse, of course, but if she did, there was a very real chance her decision could come into play when the Director of Sales and Marketing position finally became available. When that happened, it meant Adrian would go into early retirement and be out of her hair. Her official promotion was just a formality.

The draw of that moment was overwhelming.

She licked her lips, her gaze pointed at her feet. She needed a pedicure and made a mental note to take care of that as soon as possible. "Sure."

"What was that?"

Her eye roll took an exaggerated turn this time. Good thing he was not around to see it. "I said sure. I'll check in with Finn to see if he would like the grand tour."

"Don't just check in with him—make him go."

She gave him a negative little laugh. "Are you serious? Your brother is the head of a major corporation. I'm quite sure he'll know whether he has the time and the need for the tour."

"He has both. Trust me. Now, I'm signing off so you can make your plans. Let me know how it goes."

The line went quiet.

"Adrian?" Nothing.

He'd hung up. Lacy let out an exaggerated exhale.

"Was it something I said?"

Lacy yelped at the sound of Finn's voice and spun around.

He chuckled. "My apologies."

"You ... scared me."

He looked as if he had just walked up from the beach. His feet were bare, his tee perfectly tailored to hug him in the right places ... all the chiseled ones. Vaguely, she noticed his eyes travel the length of her, then correct themselves abruptly as they met her gaze. Part of her wished she had done more than put her hair up in a clip and pat some sunscreen on her skin. The other part didn't care at all.

"Out for a walk?" It was the most banal thing she could think of to say.

"Actually, I'm looking for you."

"Me?"

"My brother says you are my ticket to the grand tour of the fine town of Colibri."

Her mouth dropped open, her eyes narrowing.

"Hm. That's quite the reaction. You're not the ticket or you don't want to show me around?"

"Neither. I'm just wondering ... when did you speak to Adrian, if I might ask? We only hung up a few minutes ago."

He flashed her a bright smile that showed off his warm tan. "The Hastings brothers move fast."

She stared at him.

He cleared his throat, that smile faltering. "So. Is every-thing my brother said true? Are you the one to show me around your hometown?"

She crossed her arms and laughed, though it sounded stilted, even to her. "Considering I haven't lived here in years, I'm not sure how much I can help you." She wasn't ready to mention she had promised Adrian she'd do just that, espe-cially when a shower beckoned.

"I get the feeling this place has not changed very much over the years."

She shrugged. "You are right about that."

"And you probably still have plenty of memories of the area."

She hesitated. His dark eyes had managed to snag her, sending a warm thrill through her, though she wished that weren't the case. How would she get through this without losing her mind? Not to mention ... her heart? She unfolded her arms. "Yes. Sure. I can give you a tour of Colibri, Finn. Can you wait until noon?"

He nodded. "Absolutely. I'll see you then."

An hour later, Lacy sat on the front porch hoping she looked more serene than she felt. She wore a hibiscus-patterned sundress and sandals because she planned to make this quick. Her old camera sat in her lap. Finn's driver, "Jeevs," or Frank, or whatever, could squire them around as she gestured toward points of interest. Basically, they would make a loop, she would snap a few photos, and by her calculations, she would be back in her well-worn home by mid-afternoon.

"Ready to go?"

Lacy's heart did a somersault. Finn stood on the bottom step in a white button down, grey linen slacks, and ecru loafers, like he was about to visit a winery. "I'm ready," she said, feeling more heady than ready. "I suppose Frank will be driving, correct?"

"Incorrect."

She kept her gaze benign.

He cracked a smile and slid his shades over his eyes. "I rented a car. C'mon." He waved her toward him. Together they walked over to the driveway and he opened the door of a new BMW convertible. "Okay if I leave the top down?"

"Whatever you'd prefer." She'd never cared much about impressing anyone with her hair. If it got in her way, she could always clip it up into an easy chignon.

He pulled out of the drive. "Lead the way."

"Didn't you bring your map?"

He stopped and looked at her over his shades. "You're kidding."

She settled against the soft leather seats and flashed him a grin. "I am."

Finn stared at her for a beat, allowing his own grin to appear. "Humor. Impressive."

She gave him a little shrug and he glanced at the camera in her lap but didn't mention it.

"Go straight out of here," she said, pointing, "and then take a left at the small intersection up ahead."

"Yes, ma'am."

She knew the way by heart, having ridden her bicycle along this way dozens, maybe even hundreds of times as a kid. Lacy hadn't been down this way in years, but she had a hunch there would still be open land to consider. Of course, anyone wanting to actually develop said land might have trouble with the powers that led this one-dolphin town.

"There's a small rise up ahead," she said, "to the right."

The vacant land was mostly bare, save some spindly pine trees in a far corner. A remnant of tile steps led nowhere. Finn pulled the car to the side of the road and shut off the engine. "Shall we walk the land?"

Lacy shrugged, unbuckled her seatbelt, and lifted her door handle.

"Hold on a minute." Finn stepped out of the car and quickly walked around to Lacy's side. He pulled the door open and held it for her.

She pasted on a smile, the professional kind that she had become accustomed to whipping out the minute a potential client came into view. Nothing fake about it, but neither was it an organic smile that grew out of a longtime relationship.

Lacy's sandals slapped across the sidewalk and up the steps to nowhere. Finn followed closely behind her. She stopped when she reached the top and he bumped into her.

"Pardon me."

She threw a gaze over her shoulder. "Totally my fault. What would you like to see?"

He surveyed the property, which gave them a view of foothills to the east and a peek of ocean to the west. "I'd like to walk it a bit, get a feel for what's up here."

She shrugged. "Not much, really. It's mostly sand and the view isn't as good as the one you have at your rental, and the access is worse."

"You always so positive?"

"Just stating an opinion. I suppose it could house a nice boutique property, if you're thinking of going in a new direction with Hastings Resorts."

"Perhaps I am."

"Well, okay then." She stepped aside so he could pass. "Have a look around. I didn't wear the right shoes to go traipsing about."

"I could carry you."

She jerked a look at him, noticing the laughter lines at the corners of his eyes. "I'm good," she said.

Finn chuckled, then walked part of the perimeter of the lot. If it were for sale, Lacy had no idea. For all she knew, they were trespassing, but she doubted anyone would care. As she waited, she framed a shot of the hazy view. Then another of a small stand of trees. The familiar snap of the shutter provided a sense of familiarity, comfort even.

He wandered back and stopped at the top of the stairs. "Ready to go?" she asked.

"Ready. Let me walk on ahead of you so you don't slip."

"Are you going to catch me if I do?" As soon as the words slipped out, she wished she could stuff them back into her mouth. Had he wondered the same thing a moment ago?

"It would be to my shame if I didn't."

She bit back a smile. He was making it really tough to be annoyed with him and she had to remind herself about why she was.

They wound along the oblong-shaped trail as she pointed out the elementary school, a row of tiny houses that were once said to be part of a long-gone camp, and a sprawling park. "I often rode my bike all around here in the summers."

"Intriguing," he said.

"How so?"

"The largest playground in the world is across the street, and yet the town has designated a park within view of it."

Oh. She thought a moment. "Maybe it's because kids need structure and boundaries."

He slid a look at her, a question in his gaze.

She turned up her palms and laughed lightly. "I read that somewhere."

He nodded, still surveying the area. "Did you spend much time here as a child?"

She paused, the question feeling more personal than she might have expected. She shaded her eyes with one hand and looked up at him. "I did."

He smiled. "That's good to know."

"We were here mostly in the summertime, although my

father sometimes brought us back when he had work in the area." She shrugged. "But as I mentioned, the area has remained strangely unchanged."

"I wonder if there are homes that might be ready to be torn down."

"Hm. I'm not sure if ready is the right term for it, but I'm sure some developers would like to come in and level the place. My impression is that the townspeople frown on that sort of thing."

"I see." Finn's expression changed suddenly. He held out his hand but she hesitated. He nodded. "So you won't slip on the steps since you are wearing sandals. I apologize for not realizing earlier."

Lacy took his hand, holding it as lightly as possible. She attempted to ignore the warmth in it and the way his steady strength made her knees want to buckle.

"Where to next?" he asked when they were back in the car.

She thought a moment. She hadn't taken him to her favorite spot, the place she had often run to when she was young, and did not intend to. She gave him a questioning shrug. "I don't really know. I suppose we could drive through town, or have you already checked out the two streets that are considered the hub of the area?"

"Kidding, right?"

"I'm not."

"Never quite sure with you."

"I've done my job well then."

He chuckled. "If you say so." Finn started the car. "Lead me to the bustling downtown of Colibri."

As promised, the main part of town was all of two blocks

long. She pointed out Luke's surf shop, Giovanni's Restaurant, and Brooke's Beachside Bakery. Finn peered at the place. "Says they have espresso."

"So it does."

"Unless you're hungry for something more substantial. Sushi, perhaps?"

She winced. "No. Never."

"Doesn't like sushi. Good to know." He flipped a glance at the bakery again. "I'm game for coffee. You?"

"Why not?" She wasn't game. Not really. Lacy gave site inspections for a living—tours of the Vegas property to interested event planners—but this trip around Colibri with the head of the company had vacillated between professional courtesy and keeping herself from swooning. She hoped that had not been obvious to him.

On their way inside, they ran into Rafael. The shirtless wonder actually wore one today. He stopped and flashed a wide smile at Lacy, grabbed her hand, and kissed it. "Hey, beautiful."

"Well, hello to you too, Rafael." She turned. "I'd like you to meet Finn Hastings."

They each nodded their hellos with about as much warmth as an unheated pool in springtime.

Rafael's gaze returned to her. "Good to run into you. Maggie says you might need some help with moving furniture and other jobs around the old place. Do you have my number?"

Lacy grabbed her phone. "Great idea. I don't but give it to me and I'll be in touch."

After she'd keyed his number into her phone and said goodbye, they approached the counter.

They ordered two cappuccinos and eclairs, all the while Lacy wondering what she'd gotten herself into. The past hour felt like a dream. When was the last time a billionaire had taken her on a Sunday drive in his convertible?

That would be never. Not that she had sought out that sort of thing. She had dated, plenty of times, but men were too picky. Or maybe she was. She took a surreptitious glance at Finn as he sipped his coffee and surveyed the creampuff of a bakery they had found themselves in. Lashes for days. Had she noticed before how long his dark eyelashes were? The soberness she had always found intriguing in him, well, on the few occasions that she had actually been in the same room with Finn, had vanished. He looked tan, relaxed, and maybe even a little smitten with the small town of Colibri.

"I'm not overwhelmed," he said suddenly, breaking her reverie.

She froze. "Excuse me?"

He stirred the foam in his cup. "Impressed, but not over-whelmed."

"With Colibri?"

"Yes."

This rankled her somehow, like a personal slight, which, when you think of it, made zero sense since she had not really cared to come back here in the first place.

Lacy kept her expression calm, unfettered. It wasn't easy. Why did she suddenly care what Finn Hastings thought about where she had grown up?

He leaned forward as if pulling her into his confidence. "I do find the area charming in its own way, but I have yet to envision it as a host for one of our hotels."

"Of course."

"Am I wrong?"

She looked into his eyes, searching for a dare, as in, would she, as his subordinate, dare to tell him otherwise? For a half second, Lacy considered suggesting they make one more stop on the way back to their respective houses. No one knew the area like she did. Somehow, this thought both emboldened and shook her. Her mind wandered to the hours she would spend on her bike as a kid, zigzagging through the streets, with no one breathing down her neck to get back home.

Sometimes she wondered if anyone noticed she was gone at all.

"You're the boss," she finally said. "I believe that when you find what you're looking for, you will know it when you see it."

Finn considered her for a long moment, so long that she nearly broke eye contact with him. Finally, he nodded. "I suppose you're right."

They finished their coffees and luscious snack in a comfortable silence, and she noticed, with some surprise, that she was not looking forward to the end of their time together. Lacy lifted her gaze once or twice to find Finn watching her. Or so it seemed to her. But she would not allow herself to think that his focus on her meant anything more than it did.

He was doing his due diligence, and as the head of a thriving corporation, that was to be expected. Finn was known as a man who could be hyper-focused in business. One story that circulated around the office water coolers was the time he was in negotiations for their Chicago property when a car ran over a hydrant right outside of the all-glass conference rooms. His assistant and others in the room were agog as they watched thousands of gallons of water shoot into the street, scattering cars and people from the area. But Finn kept on with negotiations, never letting his gaze slide from the task at hand until he got what he wanted.

She thought about that. Maybe the so-called cool, calm exterior was part of his tactic all along.

Well, no matter. Finn would be leaving Colibri soon, so she too needed to stay focused. No sense in allowing her heart to take a hit. She'd already found herself falling for him once in that first brief moment of conversation a year before, but then soon realized how he treated his brother. Fool me once, shame on you. Fool me twice?

She wasn't about to let that happen.

IF LACY WAS ANYONE ELSE, he might have asked her to dinner. But how could he have done so without annihilating all protocol? Finn puffed out his cheeks and blew out a harsh breath, trying to clear his mind. No wonder his brother was attracted to Lacy. She was more than beautiful to look at— she had spirit and fire. She wasn't afraid of him, and he liked that, though he suspected she was holding back some of her fire due to his position as her, well, as her boss. Or at least, her boss's boss.

One thing he knew for sure: she complicated things for him in Colibri. And outside of Colibri as well.

Finn frowned. Was it possible that he had misread his brother's intentions? He knew that Adrian would not do anything to make Lacy uncomfortable. Even if he had feelings for her, he would have to know that those feelings were returned before he approached her about them. He thought more about this. Perhaps a call to their human resources director might be in order.

Of course, Finn could clear all this up with one simple phone call to his brother.

But would his very private, health-compromised brother reveal his true feelings?

A groan escaped him and he checked the time on his computer. After eleven. Finn had been working at the mahogany desk with the ocean view for hours, only vaguely aware of the sun's disappearance followed by the moon's eerie glow. He might have stopped earlier if the Wi-Fi had not been so glitchy, but who was he trying to kid? He was a workaholic, though he did not discount that trait as some did. Like Paige did.

He moved to close his email when he caught sight of one from Lillian Madsen. She had been making promises since Helene's first communication with her, saying she had secured—or would soon secure—the listings of several beachfront properties that his company could buy as teardowns. The draw of an oceanfront resort, especially in this rather quiet little town, was not something he could easily ignore. It would mean an entirely new spin on Hastings Resorts, and in fact, he contemplated starting another entity to brand this type of resort as such.

Ms. Madsen had laid out the general location of the homes. It was no secret that zoning laws would have to be changed, but to his mind, that was a minor blip. Along with the sweeping views, he had also seen areas of neglect in the town's infrastructure. Roads that needed repairing, medians and sidewalks that could use some trimming or replanting, and signage that had been badly battered by sand-laden wind. Certainly, his team could come up with an offer that would address those needs.

Something, however, niggled at him. The Holloway house was among the houses designated by Madsen Real Estate & Investments as an upcoming listing. And yet, Lacy had not mentioned it. He had heard about her parents' accident, and his assistant had sent her a note of condolence and flowers for the memorial.

Finn twisted his mouth, thinking. Guilt sank in his gut, like a rare stone. How had he not managed to personally offer her his condolences, especially after they had spent so much of the morning together? To acknowledge that her presence at the family beach house must come with mixed feelings?

No wonder she hadn't mentioned the possibility of the family home being designated as a tear-down. The subject was likely a sore one. Compassion flooded him and he pushed his laptop away.

After a moment, Finn stood, stretching his torso. Perhaps another reason for this long sweep at the computer was that it kept him occupied. He glanced over at the Holloway home, not able to help himself, and noticed light coming from an upstairs window. Lacy's bedroom? A night owl? Did she like to read? Work late?

The thoughts roused something in him and he stepped quickly into the kitchen, pulled open the refrigerator door and closed it just as quickly. He should have asked Frank to buy something other than coffee, milk, and wine before sending him on his way. Thankfully, he had asked the valet to pick up some dry goods for the pantry.

Finn grabbed a bag of almonds, poured himself a glass of Syrah, and walked onto the back deck. His feet were bare, his skin slightly cool after sitting in one place for so long. The red wine warmed him and he smiled. He would have liked to tell Lacy that she had drawn his attention to the wine, though doing so would reveal that she had made an impression on him from day one of their meeting. As he sipped, he wondered more about her likes, dislikes, tastes ... and what about her job in Vegas? Was she happy there? Most importantly, did she return her brother's obvious admiration for her?

He flicked a look to the south where a bonfire flared, sending sparks and the occasional pop into the air. Even from here he could feel the energy of it. Directly in front of him, a group of people milled about close to the shoreline, their voices punctuating the night. The weather, though cooling some, still held the summer's warmth in it and the revelers had noticed. If he were back in New York now, it would not be out of the ordinary to leave his apartment at this time of night in search of a late bite. Going for a walk on the beach, however, would have never entered his head.

The moon was full and the tide flowing out, so he shrugged off his reticence. After another sip, Finn set his wineglass on the table that was anchored to the deck and dashed back inside for a jacket. Foregoing shoes, he wandered down to the sand where the number of people swelled, his curiosity piqued.

He had nearly reached the crowd when he heard his name being called. Finn turned to see Lacy, her hair piled on her head with tendrils falling from it like she had just been in a windstorm. Her bare feet stuck out beneath a massive towel wrapped around her body.

"Good evening, Lacy."

"Sir."

"Sir?"

"I thought we were being formal."

He cracked a confused smile.

After a moment she said, "So you are a fan of grunion."

"Grunion?"

"That's why you're out here, isn't it?" She smiled earnestly and he had half a mind to join her inside that towel. Reluctantly, he cast a look around, a spark of something coming to him, though he couldn't exactly place it. Still, he answered, "Yes. Of course."

She hesitated, her eyes searching his face, then laughed, the sound of it a revelation. "You have no idea what I'm talking about, do you?"

He had trained himself to keep his facial expressions in check, not let the other side see his hand of cards—if he were in hard negotiations. But with her? He could not seem to wipe the silly smile from his face. "Maybe you should tell me."

A whoop or two ricocheted through the crowd, and she surprised him by dropping the towel some and hooking her arm through his, her fingers pressing gently into his flesh. She leaned in closer. "We're out here waiting for the grunion to run. If it happens, it'll be spectacular." She gave him a friendly little hug and unhooked their arms.

"Tell me more."

"This is something that happens along the coast several

times during the spring and summer months, only after high tide. You'll see thousands of shiny fish, like big sardines, come ashore. It's magnificent."

He quirked a look at her. "You've been holding out on me. What other secrets of Colibri are you keeping?"

Lacy fanned her arm in front of her. "Look at all these people. I don't think it's much of a secret."

He nodded. "Yes, actually, I believe I've heard of this, though I have never been in the right place to see it. Why do they come ashore?"

She pulled back slightly, a strange laugh coming from her. "To spawn."

"Ah. Of course."

"What do you mean 'of course'?"

"It's better than the alternative."

"Which is?"

"I thought perhaps that they were coming ashore to die."

"Oh my goodness, Finn, that's awful!"

He sputtered a laugh, all in fun, and shrugged. "What can I say? I'm a New Yorker. Late nights are for after-show dining and elevator rides to the top—not walking barefoot on the beach."

Lacy sighed. "That has got to be one of the saddest things I have ever heard."

"Oh, I don't know. Maybe you'll have a chance to try it sometime." He winked, though she might not have noticed it in the dark. Probably for the best.

"I do love New York," she finally said. "But there's something about the craziness of all of this"—she waved that hand through the air again—"that makes me realize what I may have been missing."

His gaze brushed over her face, and for a second or two, her mouth turned down, as if regret had come over her. A sudden desire to know everything behind that statement filled him. Voices rose around them, but he blocked out the sound, studying her. He, too, had a feeling that he had been missing ... something.

"Lacy," he began.

She squealed and grabbed his arm again, pulling him away from the water's edge. "It's starting, Finn! Come on!"

Chaos ensued as a sudden torrent of thousands of fish flip-flopped onto shore, alternately displaying their silvery bellies and blueish-green backs. Calls to get back and give them space controlled the crowd that rejoiced at the spectacle, laughter and awe coming from the youngest to old-timers who had shown up, as if on schedule, to watch the ritual. The sand in front of them was covered by the creatures.

Her hand continued to grip his upper arm. He resisted the urge to cover it with his own hand, to keep her from letting go. Instead, he turned his face to watch her in the moonlit night, her expression fully happy, joyful, and for a moment, he saw a flash of the little girl who had once been on this beach, laughing under the stars.

"They're so pretty!" she said, laughing.

"And frisky," another woman added.

Yeah," the woman's male companion said. "That's a lot of mating going on out there!"

Lacy snorted a little and giggled, the sound of it strangely appealing. Another break of the waves sent a rush of grunion to the beach, putting Finn and Lacy squarely in the middle of thousands of fish apparently doing their version of a mating dance. He took hold of Lacy's hand and pulled her up a slope until they landed on dry sand. He dropped onto his behind and she landed next to him.

Finn squeezed Lacy's hand and let it go, both of them laughing still. Down below them the crowd of children and adults continued to squeal and run to the outer edges of the phenomenon. She lifted her phone and snapped a round of pictures, her sighs sounding like soft squeals. Waves crashed. A breeze picked up. After a few moments, Lacy pulled her towel around herself again. He thought he heard her teeth chatter.

He moved closer to her, until their knees touched, though hers were wrapped in terry cloth. They sat there a long while watching, until the crowd dissipated and gusts of wind reminded them how very late it was. Lacy slid a look at him, her face alive with the memory of the night. Silently, she stood and Finn followed. He walked her home, the quiet between them both comfortable and full of questions.

4

———————

"Do you have a plus one?"

Lacy scrunched her entire face at Maggie's question. "Have you lost your mind?" She turned away from her sister and glanced at her cell phone as if it were a magic eight ball, a kid's game asking her a rather ridiculous question.

Maggie laughed lightly. "Don't be so easily offended. I was just asking."

"I've only been here a week!"

"You grew up here. Sort of."

"That means nothing, you know."

"Not really, it doesn't."

Lacy paused at the suspicious tone in Maggie's voice. "Spill it."

"It's nothing really. I ran into Rafael at the beach and he casually mentioned seeing you with a man at the bakery and I thought, perhaps, it might be the same guy—Finn, was it? —who showed up here the other day." She giggled but hardly took a breath. "By the way, don't mention to Luke that I was talking to our neighborhood shirtless wonder. He kinda has a thing against him."

Lacy snapped an eye roll to the ceiling. "Doesn't anyone have anything else to do around here?"

"Well?"

She shook her head. "The gossip chain is strong as ever around here."

"He said he was a *suit.* Um, wait a second. Lacy! You said his last name was Hastings. No way!"

"What?"

Maggie dipped her chin, her eyes narrowed. "Your boss didn't follow you here, right?"

"Not exactly."

Her big sister put a hand to her forehead. "How did I not realize this?"

"You're getting married. You are allowed to have bride brain."

"Ha! But you haven't answered my question. He either did or didn't follow you here, and have you reminded him that you're on sabbatical? Not to mention that you have a job to do while you're here?"

Lacy had spent the morning removing photos, doodads, and anything else deemed too personal from the bedroom on the first floor. She ran her thumb along a photo of her and her siblings sitting under Maggie's blue umbrella— Maggie looked curvy, Grace smart, Jake bored, and Bella otherworldly. The expression on her own face was more difficult to describe. It was a mix between anticipation and disappointment and she really wished she could recall what had been happening on that particular day. Or if that was just her regular face.

She sighed and set the photo back down on the old whale bedspread. "If you must know, my boss's boss, which actually makes him the big boss, has rented the house next door—which, by the way, is a big secret, so shush. Anyway, he is here to scout land and I was asked to give him a tour of Colibri. That's it."

"So it's a big secret because of competitors?" Maggie laughed. "I doubt seriously there are any, not that Colibri isn't a hidden gem, in my opinion."

"No. Wren told me that a local group of homeowners are against vacation rentals, so she asked me not to mention that the one next door to ours is being used in that way. She also, quite coincidentally, asked me to bring the key over when Finn arrived."

"Huh."

"Huh, what?"

"I don't really think there's such a thing as coincidence."

"I'm not lying to you, Mags. She asked me to bring the key over to the evening arrival and it happened to be Finn Hastings."

Maggie sucked in air. "Oh! *The* Finn Hastings? He's a ... billionaire."

"Duh. So is your brother. You knew I was working for Hastings Resorts, right? What's your point?"

"I hadn't actually made the connection, Lacy, but now that you ask, I don't know what to think. You've been seen around town with a hot billionaire, something you've kept a secret until now, and I'm supposed to believe the whole thing is accidental? I know my degree is only in hair—"

"Don't go there. No one in this family has ever looked down on you for being a hairstylist. Thanks for the trim, by the way."

"You're welcome and I know that. I'm just saying that despite my lack of a college education, I'm smart enough to know when something doesn't add up."

Lacy laughed lightly now. "I don't know what you want me to say. Everything I've told you is the truth."

Maggie was silent for several long seconds. "Okay."

Lacy shot a look at her sister. "Okay, really?"

"Yes. If you say you've told me everything, then, fine."

"Great. Let's get back to the topic of your wedding."

"Oh, Lacy, I can't wait to marry Luke." Her sister's voice turned pliable. She didn't know whether to smile or gag a little. "After the ceremony, we're hosting a small dinner at Giovanni's. They make fabulous Italian food and I know it's going to be fun—I'm so glad you'll be there."

"You know what? I'm happy too. It'll be something I can always hang over the rest of the family."

"Oh stop it."

Lacy smiled.

"Now about that plus one—"

Lacy gasped. "Are we back to that?"

"Listen, there is room, so if you decide you want to invite someone, please do. That's all I'm going to say on the matter."

"Well," Lacy said, "I guess I could always ask Rafael if he's available. Didn't he accompany Daisy to a wedding not too long ago?"

"Yes, he did, and Jake's still annoyed about it. And I've already told you why this would be a bad idea."

Lacy laughed. Rafael managed to get under the skin of at least two of the men in the family. That took some talent. She finished up her call with Maggie and went back to reorganizing the bedroom. Everything had come off the walls, but when she surveyed her work, she frowned. Either she would have to patch and paint like crazy or find other suitable and non-personal art to close up all those holes.

She twisted her mouth. Even if she were to cover them up with new pieces, she would always know those holes were there. And it would drive her crazy.

Reluctantly, Lacy slipped into her shoes and headed outside to the garage. She lifted the garage door, making a mental note that an actual garage door opener would be a key upgrade to finally pull the old house into the twenty-first century, and searched for her father's tool chest.

She was rifling through it, looking for something to spread spackling paste onto the walls with, when she heard a throat clear. Lacy jumped.

"My apology." Finn stood at the opening of the garage, a warm smile on his face. He looked relaxed in an untucked button-down shirt, one hand stuck into the pocket of his shorts, and his eyes guarded by a pair of sunglasses. "I didn't mean to scare you once again."

"It's no problem." She shut the toolbox lid and headed toward him. "You look rested."

"Nothing like wearing myself out chasing grunion."

She laughed at that. "We'll make a Californian out of you yet." She glanced at his leather sandals, which were looking rather pitted from the sand. "Next thing you know, you'll be picking up a pair of flip-flops at Luke's surf shop."

Finn laughed heartily at this. "Don't hold your breath."

She reached up to close the garage door and Finn stepped forward, placing his hands above her. "Here, let me."

Lacy blinked, unaccustomed to chivalry. The few men she dated—and she was quite picky—were inconsistent, sometimes offering to open her car door and other times too preoccupied with the phone in their hands to notice her still sitting next to them. Headiness washed over her and she had to remind herself that this was an extraordinary situation: He was her boss and here in Colibri for information—and that was it.

"I've had more time to think about that spectacle last night," he said, "and I really do believe you have been holding out on me."

She looked up at him, squinting in the sunlight, her own reflection staring back at her through his lenses. "Hm. How so?"

"Well, for one thing, I spotted the bicycle in the garage and that reminded me that you mentioned riding all over the place. Surely there is more to show me than where you took me yesterday."

Didn't he have a real estate agent to show him around? She thought it, but didn't say it out loud as that might sound like insubordination. Then again, she wasn't on the clock right now. Last night had deluded her into thinking that maybe she and Finn had evolved past a professional relationship. Neither had expected to run into the other, but when they had, neither left the other's side.

But then he walked her home with nothing but a rather impersonal goodbye. And that was that.

"You look busy."

She glanced at the scraper in her hand and realized that

she had completely forgotten to dig around for the spackling paste that Maggie had left in the garage. Lacy slipped some wayward strands of hair behind her ear. "Just puttering around today."

"If you're free, I would like you to take me to some of your favorite spots."

There's only one, really.

He continued, "We can pick up some espresso for the drive." He paused. "Have I convinced you yet?"

"I do have a favorite spot, but I'd hate to see it turned into a hotel."

His eyes darkened, but she felt emboldened somehow.

"It might change someday, but I'd like to remember it the way it's always been."

He nodded. "I can respect that. Will you show it to me?"

A small piece of the crust on her heart broke away. She shrugged, though there was a good-naturedness to it. "Sure. Let me clean up and I'll meet you back here in fifteen minutes."

As promised, after she dashed inside to brush her hair, line her lips, and grab her old camera off of a shelf, Lacy met Finn outside. She'd taken those few minutes to think about whether to show him her favorite place in Colibri, and as she did, her mind flung back to last night again.

Several times during the spontaneous grunion run, Lacy had caught unfettered joy on Finn's face. With his money and connections, she knew he had access to yachts and ski chalets and, well, beachfront homes. And yet, he had laughed like a little boy and lingered out on that beach, watching a show that was free for everyone who experienced it.

Maybe her favorite, most sacred spot in Colibri would be safe with him.

For the second time this week, Finn drove with the top down on his car. Lacy's long hair whipped around her, accentuating the freedom she felt as he whisked her through the foothills. He glanced at her more than once, sending a decided chill through her—the good kind—and for the first time in a very long while, Lacy felt anything but invisible.

They were just about to miss the turn when she gestured for him to slow down. The driveway was nearly hidden by overgrown bushes and a median filled with weeds.

He slowed to a crawl and craned his neck, looking for where to turn. "Here?"

He sounded skeptical and she second-guessed herself. Finn was staring at her, waiting for an answer, though, so she nodded quickly and he made the sharp turn. He whistled and put the car in a lower gear. Lacy shut her eyes, remembering. She had not been up to this spot in many years, and yet she expected—and fully hoped—that it had remained unchanged.

Finn gasped. He looked at her, another whistle escaping him. "Wow."

As for her, a smile burgeoned on her face, one she could not control. She could feel it. From her cursory glance, it appeared that the land had remained virtually unchanged, except for new growth on the bushes and trees. From the looks of things, nothing had been thinned out. The trees and garden were thick with undergrowth and the house still wore a faded coat of cottage blue.

Finn parked the car and, wordlessly, they both exited. She looped her camera strap over her head and let the camera itself rest against her body. The land stretched flat and wide, one corner to the next, no sign of any other property beside them. There was a 360-degree view, nearly half of it facing the ocean.

He came to stand beside her, his eyes questioning. Instinctively, she knew what he wanted to ask. That alone amazed her.

She flicked a glance around and returned her gaze to him. "You want to know how I managed to get up here on my bicycle."

He exhaled a chuckle. "I have no doubts about your athletic ability."

"Of course not."

Another chuckle escaped him. "However, yes, I was wondering what kind of drive a teen would have to have in order to pedal all the way up here. That was some hill."

This was harder to answer. The view might have been answer enough, but she knew that it wasn't all there was. She began to walk, to drag the toe of her shoe on the gravel driveway. Lacy could recall the times that she would jump on her bike and pedal around Colibri for hours at a time. She had passed this driveway often, but had always been warned to avoid it.

Then one day, she rolled back into her garage and her father looked up. "Are you going out on a bike ride, Lacy?"

He never meant to hurt her. He just hadn't noticed that she had been gone. With five children piled up around the house, was that any surprise?

Lacy turned around to find Finn watching her, her mind brought back to the present. She gave him a small shrug. "I don't know, exactly. I would just ... just get lost for a while, and then one day, I decided to make the climb up here to see what I could find."

"Quite the find."

"Yes, it is."

"Do you know who owns it?"

She quirked a smile at him. "No, I don't."

"Well, I would hate to be arrested for trespassing."

She smiled wider now. "I doubt that would happen."

"Because you're one of the beloved townspeople?"

She scoffed. "Not at all. Hardly anyone knows me around here." Lacy gestured toward the house. "Word is there's a ghost in that house. He or she or whatever owns this place."

Finn gave her a questioning look.

"Well, that's what I've always heard."

He crossed his arms and one of his brows shot upward. "Do you believe in ghosts?"

She thought about this. Two boys had told her the ghost story when she was about twelve. It intrigued her, but believe it? She looked at him. "Not really."

What *was* important to her was that those boys—and everyone else around here—believed in it. Because it kept them away. Not that she didn't help perpetuate the myth at times …

He nodded. "Me neither."

She laughed and reached for his arm, pulling him along. Alarm bells went off inside her head, warning her that grabbing hold of her boss's arm might not be the wisest thing to do. She ignored them.

"Here's where I carved my initials into a tree." She pointed at the gnarled trunk of a tree that had arched itself in the wind, yet stayed rooted all these years.

"Sounds romantic."

"Um, no. I carved only *my* own initials."

He chuckled. "Wow. That's sad."

She shrank back in mock offense and added a little gasp for emphasis.

He pulled off his shades and looked directly at her. "Are you trying to tell me that you did not have boys lining up to add their initials next to yours?"

"Oh brother."

He continued to hold his gaze on her. "Was Rafael otherwise occupied that day?"

This time when she sputtered it was not put on. "Oh my gosh. What?"

He shrugged. "It is not difficult to imagine you as a teenager with a posse following after you."

"And you think Rafael was one of them."

"I saw the way he looked at you."

Lacy had heard everything now. What was he saying ... why was he mentioning Rafael? She shook her head. In some small way, she wished that what he suggested was true. But it wasn't. No one really noticed her back then. Not her family, not guys ... not anyone. She had thought about this more than once but had never had a conversation about it with her sisters or anyone who might have insight. The truth was, she had felt this way for most of her life—including at Hastings Resorts. She had been promised a promotion, but after a year, it had not materialized.

Lacy glared at him, suddenly annoyed. And exposed. Why did she bring him up here?

He continued, though his dark brows had dipped some. "Sore subject. I apologize."

"It's not a sore subject because it's not a subject at all. Everyone around here knows Rafael because he's one of the few from my age group who has stuck around. I don't know what you think you saw, but you misinterpreted him."

"I've upset you."

She sighed and leaned against that tree, suddenly feeling silly about the initials, this conversation ... even about bringing him here. "Not upset. I'm just ... tired of everything."

There was a shift in his countenance, a further darkening in his expression. Finn stepped closer to her. "Tell me what you're feeling."

Slowly she gazed up at him, expecting to see at least a hint of mockery. Instead, there was a certain earnestness in his features, his brown-black eyes affixed on hers, his speech suspended. Lacy had the distinct sense that Finn wanted to reach out to her.

Or was that because she wanted to reach out to him?

The truth was ... she did. If he wasn't *the* Finn Hastings, wasn't the head of her company—a man who could have any woman he wanted—then she might have leaned into these feelings that were about to undo her. She sensed a quickening in her breath, a catch in her throat. If only she could tell him really what she was feeling.

He stared at her for a few seconds longer and then turned toward the expanse of sky that hovered over the sea. The moment disappeared and she began to question herself, to wonder if what she had felt had any place in her reality at all.

"I can see why you love this place," he finally said, turning his gaze back to her. "I think I'm falling ... too."

She licked her lips, her throat suddenly dry, and forced herself to say, "It's beautiful in many ways to me."

He reached above her and leaned his arm against the tree trunk. "I can see that." He gazed at her, the silence heavy, her own heart beating in her ears. Whatever worries she'd had about him in the past, even the recent past, had vanished. His eyes brushed over her face and lingered on her mouth. He pressed his lips together then, and slowly pushed himself away from the tree, pulling his gaze away from her and folding his arms at his chest.

Lacy took a step backward and nearly stumbled. He turned and reached out for her, but she flashed both palms. "I'm okay."

He watched her, conflict moving across his face. A few seconds passed and he stepped back too, a resigned sigh in his voice. "Thank you for taking the time to show me around up here, Lacy. I appreciate it."

She nodded.

"Ready to head back?"

She wasn't. But she pasted on the smile that had helped her book hundreds of events over the years and followed Finn back to the car.

HE COULD NOT GO on this way. Finn tried to open his email for the umpteenth time this morning, but the glitchy Wi-Fi had finally sputtered to a near stop. Trying to open a browser felt akin to being stuck behind a student driver when late for a meeting.

Finn shut his laptop. He stood and paced, his mind a

tangle of unfinished thoughts. Part of him wanted to land on Lacy's front porch, pull her into his arms, and stay there until sunset. The other wanted to avoid her with everything he had.

Either way, he had lost the battle. He flicked a look at the modem by the fireplace, a red light in place of the one that should have been green. The bakery in town probably had Wi-Fi he could use. That's it. He would pull himself together and head into town for some unencumbered work. Anything to get his mind off of ... her.

Minutes later, he headed outside, computer case under his arm.

"Well, hello there, Mr. Johnson."

An elderly woman with salt-and-pepper curls blocked his car with her walker on wheels. A nurse stood next to her. He would not have known her if she had not called him by his pseudonym.

He put out his hand. "Hello. Call me Finn."

The old woman lifted her chin and looked him fully in the face. She shook his hand with more strength than he had predicted. "And I am Wren. I'm terribly sorry I couldn't meet you when you checked in. I-I don't get around too well anymore."

"That's quite all right. Ms. Holloway was right on time."

"Lovely! I knew she would be. I asked her to give you a map with my phone number on it. Is there anything you need?"

He smiled. "Yes, I received the map, and no, thank you. The home is nearly perfect. The Wi-Fi is the only issue I'm having, but in fact, I am on my way to the bakery right now to use theirs."

The nurse winced. "Oh dear. I'm afraid theirs doesn't work too well, either. Casualty of the beach area."

He frowned. What year was this? How could a town—any town—not have powerful enough Wi-Fi?

Wren's expression brightened. "Have you tried asking Lacy to use hers? Her brother Jake—he will be my son-in-law soon—did something in there to make theirs work better. I think it involved wires or something."

Finn pressed his mouth into a smile. "Thank you for the tip. I will be sure to ask her."

"Wonderful! Now if there is anything at all that we can help you with, I hope you will call."

"Absolutely."

He watched Wren and her nurse continue their walk. Reluctantly, he turned toward Lacy's. He really did have several important emails to answer. No doubt, given her relationship with the company, she would understand his urgent need for decent Wi-Fi.

Finn found himself on Lacy's porch. He hesitated.

"Were you going to knock or just stand there like a stalker?"

"Pardon me?"

Lacy stared at Finn through the screen door. "I heard a noise on the porch and there you were, stoic. Kind of creepy, Finn."

He scowled. "I was trying to decide whether to bother you."

"Bother me about what?"

"My Wi-Fi is ... out and I have several important emails with attachments that I need to review."

"A billionaire like you doesn't have a hot spot?"

Finn sighed. "Have I done something to offend you, Lacy? Because if I have, I would like to address it right now."

She wrinkled her forehead and then relaxed. He thought he detected an eye roll—a brief and somewhat controlled roll of her eyes.

Lacy unlatched the door. "C'mon in, boss."

He continued to watch her as he stepped inside.

"Make yourself comfortable. The table is a bit out of order at the moment, but you can sit at the island or on the couch. I'll airdrop you access."

"Thanks." He headed for the island and stopped. Every inch of the dining room table was covered in photographs. "May I?" he asked, before approaching.

She shrugged. "They're just old photos. Found them in a box and wondering which ones to keep. If any."

He stepped closer, taking in the organized mess. Shots of waves, seabirds, kids on the beach, surfers ... a couple dozen photos were fanned out as if they had been stacked together.

"Are you one of these kids?"

She didn't even look at them. "Nope."

"But they are relatives of yours, correct?"

She turned to scrutinize the photos and released a minute sigh. "Yes. Those are my siblings, actually. I have four of them—three sisters and a brother."

"A busy house. I suppose you're the youngest, then?"

"What makes you think that?"

"Well, for one thing, you do look quite young." He turned to see if she was properly flattered. By the frown on her face, he deemed that she wasn't. "And for another, you're not in any of the family photos."

"I'm in some of them somewhere." Her hand fluttered in

the air, like the Queen's wave. "I'm not the youngest, by the way—my sister Bella is. Most of the photos are of Jake and Maggie, because they got here first. They're not too far apart in age. Then there are some with the babies—my sisters Grace and Bella."

"Ah, so you're a middle kid."

"That is what they call me."

He plucked a photo from the stack, unable to take his eyes off her face. "This is one of you, isn't it?" She was much younger—probably still a teen—and wearing no makeup at all, but he recognized her by the searing eyes and the half-smile.

"Good eye there."

"You know, it almost looks like a selfie."

"That's because it is a selfie. I was taking them before they were cool."

He stared at it for a long while, until he felt her shift beside him. "It's more than that, though. This photo is quite editorial, like a story ready to be told."

She nodded, her expression telling him she was a bit confused, though likely intrigued.

He wished he could take it home with him, to scrutinize it more. But he didn't want to embarrass her. Finally, he said, "You took this with a regular camera?"

She tilted her head. "All of these were taken with my camera, some by me and some by my parents. iPhones were barely a thing and I wasn't able to buy one right away, but my aunt gave the camera to me as a gift. It became the communal camera."

"Communal. That's funny."

"As in, it disappeared from my nightstand on a regular

basis. Actually, I know that I took a lot of selfies and I'm pretty sure that I had them all developed." She shrugged. "Not sure where they all ended up, though."

He put the photo back onto the table and picked up another. He recognized the house right away, although it was in much better shape when the photo was taken. "This is the ghost house."

Lacy gave him a half smile. "It is."

The world had become so glutted with photos taken by amateurs that certain ones had begun to stand out. "You have a great eye," he said. "Not sure what it is, exactly, but there's an emotional component to some of these. Do you have formal training?"

"If you consider a half-year of photography classes in high school formal, then yes."

"Why not a full year?"

Her expression faltered and she let her gaze move away from his. She shrugged as if it didn't matter. Finally, she said, "We moved, so I wasn't able to continue."

"Not in college either?"

"I studied business and that served me well."

She had closed up, a wall now in place. Finn set the photo down, and when he did, their hands brushed. It took utter force of will not to fold his fingers over her hand and pull her into his arms. He focused on the table full of photos and in some way felt closer to her, like he could see more of who she was now and who she had been. He wanted to know more—needed to learn everything about her. Why had she moved? Where had she gone? What had happened to her between those lazy summers here in Colibri Beach and now?

Lacy stepped away from the table and pulled her hair into a sleek ponytail, holding it back with a hair tie she had been wearing around her wrist. She plucked her phone off of the counter and sent him Wi-Fi access. "Did you get it?"

"Yes. Got it."

"Okay. I have to run upstairs for a moment, but feel free to work as long as you want."

She disappeared down the hall and soon he heard footfalls as she climbed stairs. For the second time in minutes, he had to resist the urge to go after her.

Instead, he settled onto a stool at the kitchen island. It would be less comfortable than the couch, and he preferred it that way. She was driving him crazy and the best thing he could do for himself was to pack up and get out of there as fast as possible. Being uncomfortable would help in that regard.

For the next twenty minutes, he pored over a contract Helene had sent him for a massive remodel of their Chicago property. More money than he had poured into a property in years, but if the data he was relying on was correct—and it had proven to be with past endeavors—the return on his investment would be plentiful. After he looked over the contract, he forwarded it on to his attorney with his requests for changes. Undoubtedly, his lawyer would have some of his own.

He knew the minute she had returned.

"Sorry to have bothered you," she said when he turned around.

He chuckled. "You were actually very quiet."

"My brother Jake taught me that. He was an expert in sneaking out of the house as a teenager."

Finn smiled at that. "Sounds like a character. I would like to meet him someday."

"Maybe if you decide to build a resort in California, he could be your guy."

"Maybe so." He noticed a large square table he hadn't seen before. "Did you carry that downstairs?"

She looked to the side. "Oh this? Yes. It was in the upstairs master bedroom, but I think it could work down here better."

He hopped off the stool. "Here. Let me help you with that."

She waved her hands. "Actually, it's fine. I called Rafael while I was upstairs and he says he can come by tomorrow and help me move some things and to do a few other projects around here."

"I see." What kind of *other* projects ...?

Her eyes narrowed. "Do you have a problem with Rafael?"

"I don't know him."

"Exactly."

"Listen, you have been quite gracious to me, Lacy, showing me around ... sharing your Wi-Fi. I would be happy to save you the money of hiring someone and help you myself."

"I appreciate that very much, Finn, but really, it's already set. Anyway, now that I'm back downstairs, I'm going to pack up those photos again. I don't need any help with that."

He stuck a hand into the pocket of his shorts, frustrated. "Okay, if you're certain."

"I am."

"Lacy?"

She looked at him over her shoulder. "Yes?"

"Would it be possible for me to have the photo of the ghost house?"

She cracked a smile. "Stop calling it that."

He smiled back. "I will if you'll let me have it. Or let me make a copy of it." He paused. "As a memento of my time here in Colibri."

She plucked it from the bunch and held it out to him. "It's yours."

Finn took it, his eyes on her. He noticed the way she handed it to him nonchalantly, and yet the way her eyes flickered and her expression deepened, he wondered if he had hit an exposed nerve.

"Thank you." He glanced at his watch. "I have a meeting now, so I'll get out of your hair. I appreciate the use of your internet."

"Of course."

He took the stairs down her porch two at a time, regretting that he had a meeting with Lillian Madsen in a few minutes. He would rather use this time to call Adrian and talk to him, once and for all, about Lacy. Let him know what he's thinking, how he was falling hard for the brown-eyed woman who had given up some of her vacation time for him.

He stopped. Would things have been different for Finn if Brad had come clean with him about his feelings for Paige? Or what if she had told Finn that she had fallen out of love with him, but loved his best friend instead? Could their friendship have weathered that tempest?

Finn ran a hand roughly through his hair. For once, he didn't care to don a suit or put product in his waves to force them back. He decided to show up in shorts and flip-flops and see what the Realtor with a reputation had to say.

A short time afterward, Finn strolled into Madsen Real Estate & Investments intending to do more listening than speaking.

"Mr. Hastings, I am Lillian Madsen. It is a pleasure to finally meet you in person." She gripped his hand and shook it once. "Please. Sit down."

She continued. "How are you enjoying that fabulous beach house I found you?"

"Very much. Thank you."

"Excellent! I appreciate you waiting until I came back to town."

"Not a problem. I have managed to find my way around Colibri."

"A little birdie told me you have had your own personal tour guide."

He did not respond to this. He had to give her credit, though. She looked undeterred by his lack of response.

"Now, before we go any further"—she scrolled through what appeared to be a list of properties on her iPad—"I wanted to ask if you have had the chance to see inside the Holloway property? And the one on the other side of it? That one is currently owned by Wren Mcafee."

Why would that matter? He leaned forward. "I have been inside the Holloway family home to borrow the Wi-Fi. By the way, the signal is very weak in the property I am renting."

She picked up a gold pen and wrote something on a pad of paper. "Noted." She set the pen down. "Well, I suppose you heard about the terms of Lacy's parents' will. The Holloways were lovely people, certainly, but quite eccentric."

"Fascinating."

She smiled. "Did your employee not tell you about their stipulations before they are free to sell?"

"My employees' lives are private. They are not required to divulge personal information to us."

"Spoken like an upright business owner." She cackled. "I won't mention what I've heard about Lacy and that rascal Rafael either then."

Finn leveled a look at her.

She continued, as if unbothered by his silence. "Since the Holloway home is one of a number of properties that I think you will want to consider, I believe it is in your best interest to know the details surrounding its availability. Lacy may not have mentioned this, but she is here to fulfill her part of her parents' will's stipulations."

Interesting. Lacy had made no mention of selling her family's beach house. Nor had she said anything about why she was here at all. He assumed she was on vacation, or perhaps, tending to the details of the family's shared home. Hence, the rearranging of furniture. If she wasn't here for downtime—which he had already severely interrupted— what exactly was she doing here in Colibri Beach?

"I am aware of work being done around the home," he said. "But perhaps you aren't aware of the scope of the project that Hastings Properties is considering."

"Oh, I am quite aware." She leaned forward and lowered her voice in a conspiratorial way. "This may sound difficult to believe, Finn, but there are very few oceanfront resorts in California. Oh, there are many with ocean views, but not many right on the sand. At least, not of the caliber of Hastings Resorts!"

Finn knew this. The data had surprised him, had prompted him to move California up on his list of possibilities, in fact. He looked directly at Lillian Madsen. "Tell me what you propose."

LACY LAY ON THE FLOOR, photos all around her. She groaned, the act of taking a breath painful. She had suffered a back spasm and fallen, dropping the mementos of her childhood pastime with her. Now they lay scattered around her, the house in utter chaos.

Despite the pain, she cracked a smile. Her mother had used the phrase when trying to wrangle the kids—all five of them—into doing their chores. "This house is in utter chaos!" she would proclaim. They were a mangy bunch for sure, and she wondered why they had scattered to different cities as they had. Like the photos all around her.

A groan escaped her again, the threat of another spasm keeping her from trying to move. Why hadn't she just let Finn help her when he'd offered? Rafael hadn't shown up— the flake—and though it was against her better judgment to try to carry so many awkward-shaped items down the stairs, especially the heavy ones, she had been too impatient to wait another day. So she ended up on the floor.

It wasn't the first time, though hardly anyone knew. She had experienced occasional back pain from a young age. As a kid, she would curl up in bed with a book, but as she grew, she found wine and a lounge chair to be her medicine of choice.

Lacy stretched her neck to see the clock in the kitchen.

Seven-thirty already. Great. Tomorrow she would host a call with her siblings to discuss how things were moving forward and what did she have to show them? Basically, nothing.

A couple of knocks rattled the screen door. She closed her eyes. "What is it?"

"Lacy?"

Her eyes snapped open. Finn? Great …

"Everything okay in there?"

"Hold on." She pulled herself up into an almost-sitting position, gingerly sucking in air and tensing her core as she did. A light sheen of perspiration broke across her skin. "Okay," she said, trying to sound normal. "Door is unlocked."

Finn stepped inside, took a look at her, and rushed over. He squatted down until his eyes, warm and worried, were inches from hers. "You don't look well."

"Gee, thanks, boss."

He smiled, though suspicion shone in those eyes of his. "May I help you up?"

Lacy pressed her mouth shut and shook her head. If he yanked her up too fast, she could pull her back out worse. She couldn't dare. "I got it."

Quietly, Finn stood, giving her space.

She rolled to one side, lifted her arms slightly, and braced her hands on that end table she'd brought down earlier from her parents' old bedroom but never actually moved into place. With an unladylike grunt, Lacy pushed herself into a standing position, slowly, and released the breath she'd been holding. She lifted her gaze to meet his.

Round, concerned eyes stared back at her. "What happened to you? Did you … fall?"

"It's not important."

Finn crossed his arms and surveyed the room. "It is important—*you* are important, Lacy."

A lump formed in her throat and she looked away again. Tears? Really? She thought she had more control than that, but for some reason, unshed emotion sprang to her eyes. She tried hard to push the tears back.

"Hey," Finn said, reaching for her. "Let me help you to the couch."

"Not the couch." She gasped.

He raised his eyebrows, still gazing at her.

She winced. "Too soft."

He nodded and glanced around the room, stopping on the old wing chair. "If I give you some pillows for your back, would the chair work?"

She nodded, the pain keeping her from answering. Or maybe it was the tears forming. Lacy could not recall the last time she had been hovered over like this. Or if she ever had.

"Can I get you anything? Something to drink? Another pillow?"

"No, please. I'm fine." Lacy shook her head, relief making its way down her spine. "Really."

He stared at her for a long beat before stalking into the kitchen where he found an open bottle of red wine, poured a glass, and brought it to her. "Here's what is going to happen: I am going to move whatever furniture you would like to have moved."

She opened her mouth. "But—"

He held up a hand, stopping her. "Sorry. You don't have a say in this."

"Oh really."

"Really." He bent down until they were eye to eye. His voice low and husky. "You have helped me this week, now let me help you."

"You're my boss."

"Right now, you're mine." Something in his voice simmered.

Lacy swallowed back any sort of reply. His grin grew and he snapped into position, starting with the wayward end table. He lifted it like it was an empty grocery bag. "Where would you like this?"

She groaned.

He frowned.

"See, I want to put it next to the couch, but first I need to move the couch. Of course, I could just wait—"

"No." He put down the end table and stepped toward the couch. "Where do you want this?"

"I want to turn the back toward the north wall but move it far enough away from the center of the room so that one could both see through the west window and easily turn to see the front door."

He shoved the couch into the new position and plopped down on it, moving his chin right and then left. "One can."

"Excuse me?"

"See out the window and then toward the doorway. One ... can."

Lacy laughed. "Oh."

"What's next?"

"Well, I was thinking of trying that end table on the west end, but I might change my mind so—"

He put up his hand as a stop sign again. "Ah-ah-ah. Drink your wine."

She took a sip, dutifully.

"I'll give it a try and if you don't like the way it looks, I will move it for you. Capiche?"

Lacy went silent. This catering to her every whim was going to take some getting used to. But she was willing to try, especially when he used Italian on her. It reminded her of, well, home.

For the next forty-five minutes, Lacy directed Finn to grab furniture pieces from various spots in the house—upstairs and in bedrooms—and place them strategically in the great room. His lighter side was showing, in spades. "How do you like it here, darling?" he'd said more than once.

And she would answer him, "Over there, dear."

She watched him moving pieces, then looking to her for direction, then moving them again. At one point, he showed mock exasperation and flopped onto the couch, as if in protest. His hair, usually styled to smooth perfection, had shaken loose into waves. His tee clung to his chest, his biceps full from use.

A new kind of tension flowed through her. Her back had relaxed some, and she no longer feared another spasm. At the moment, she feared nothing at all.

Finn stood. Was he planning to leave? Did she dare to hope that he wouldn't? She knew then, undeniably, that she had a crush on Finn. Could he read that in her? Her own readings on him were mixed, at best. She'd felt a new warmth from him at the grunion run the other night. Even thought he might have feelings for her that she hadn't detected before.

Or maybe it was simply the sea that had brought on a change in his demeanor. Maybe some time away from

Manhattan had cured the soberness of Finn Hastings. The beach had a way of doing that to even the most uptight people—not that she would ever have described him that way.

He stretched lightly. "Mind if I join you with some wine?"

"Not at all. Please do."

He pulled another wineglass from the cupboard and poured himself a drink. He brought the bottle over to her. "A refresher?"

She nodded. After another sip, she eyed the couch. "I think I'd like to try moving to the couch."

"You're sure?"

"Yes."

"Because you want to make sure you like the new positioning before you let your servant leave the castle?"

She cracked a smile. "Something like that."

He stood and offered her his arm. "Careful, okay?"

"Yes, sir." She put her wineglass down onto the newly placed end table. Slowly, she pushed herself up with one hand and latched onto his arm with the other. No sign of a spasm, although a lingering soreness caused her to move at the pace of a tortoise.

Lacy lowered herself to the couch and stuffed a pillow behind her back. Finn watched her with anticipation and she frowned at him.

"In pain?" he asked.

"No. I need my wine."

He laughed as he grabbed it from the table and brought it to her. "Your Highness."

She bit her lip but couldn't stop smiling. "Would you mind handing me my phone as well?"

"Certainly." After he had retrieved her phone, Finn took a seat dangerously next to her, glass in hand, and for a few minutes they sat there in the quiet, watching the sun set on the horizon. The moment felt both intimate and off-limits, but she leaned into it anyway, less embarrassed than she should have been when a ripple of a sigh flowed from her.

He sighed too and she followed the sound of it. Finn was staring out the window, the sky showing off in shades of pink and orange. She picked up her phone, focused, and took his photo.

He turned, his gaze brushing over her lightly, no mention of the paparazzi picture she had just taken. "How long do you plan to stay in Colibri?"

"I'm here for another two weeks."

"Do you usually spend your vacations rearranging the furniture?"

"The short answer to that is no." One of her walls was crashing down. "But I'm not exactly on vacation."

He continued to watch her, more questions in his gaze.

She continued. "My parents were beautiful people, but eccentric in some ways. After they passed away we learned they had given most of everything they had to charity—except this house."

"They left it to you, then?"

"Sort of. Well, yes. But with a catch. Each of us—there are five in all—has to spend one month in the house before we can sell it. Otherwise, it goes to charity. Hasn't been easy with our work schedules, but so far, four of us have managed to take a month."

"That's why you took a sabbatical."

"Yes. We all decided that we would make changes to the

house with the idea of selling it after our sentence was paid."
She laughed, knowing how absurd that statement must
sound. The more time she spent in Colibri, the more she had
asked herself why she ever left. "Anyway, Grace made a list of
what needed to be done. Jake floored us all by replacing the
kitchen. Maggie painted the worst places, and I've been
doing some staging."

"Ah. The reason for the photo and furniture
rearranging."

"Yes. Exactly. I was supposed to take the last month, but
my sister Bella asked me to switch with her."

One of his brows lifted. "So you weren't supposed to be
here this month?"

"I wasn't."

Silence fell between them. She hadn't thought about the
original plan and how very different her time at the house
would have been if Bella had been here instead of her.
Suddenly, in the quiet, Lacy felt ... self-conscious.

"I am very glad you decided to switch places." He put
down his glass of wine.

She allowed her eyes to meet his, to stay there and let
him see her. She licked her lips, allowing her gaze to drop
briefly to his mouth before snapping back to his eyes. "So,
you're saying you don't like my sister."

He grinned, widely, and gently took her face in his
hands, sending a sizzle through her. "What I'm saying is I am
glad I am here—with you. Only you."

He kissed her then, that sizzle turning into a flame. She
didn't pull away, wanting him as much as he did her. He
overwhelmed her, shocked her, his kiss a combination of
tenderness and passion, of surprise and familiarity.

Lacy sank beneath the waters, submerged in ... the kiss. Her boss, her crush—Finn Hastings was kissing her.

He pulled away from her, his hands still cupping her face, his fingers entangled in her hair, his expression momentarily stunned. Finn offered her a soft smile and tipped his forehead to meet hers. "What have you gotten me into, Ms. Holloway?" he whispered.

"I can't say that I know, Mr. Hastings."

He sighed and kissed her nose before pulling farther away from her. He eyed her, though, the look of it dangerous. "You tempt me."

"Is that so bad?"

Finn ran a hand through his hair, roughly. He wore a smile, though there was a certain sadness to it that she couldn't completely decipher. Did he regret kissing her? Did he want to leave? Worse, was he worried she would call foul since he was, technically, her boss?

"What about ... my brother?"

"Your ... oh. Adrian?"

He nodded.

Finn was worried about his brother, how he would be able to handle things if she were to leave the Vegas property. "I don't know what to say."

Finn looked away, blowing out a breath. He returned his gaze to her. "Tell me I'm all wrong. Tell me you aren't committed to him."

"Committed to the hotel, you mean. Of course, I am." Did she dare mention the promised promotion? If she did, would he misconstrue her interest in him?

Finn look pained. He ran his palm down his face, slowing near his mouth, as if thinking about the ... kiss. Was he uneasy now? Lacy had not been this conflicted in, well, she couldn't remember. She had made it her policy to be straightforward, to go after what she wanted, to seize the moment.

Except when it came to Finn. Since the moment they had connected on the porch next door, she had been confused, caught up in what-ifs and other possibilities. Her eyes had been dazzled, but she had kept herself poised to run the other way. Her heart wasn't ready to become invisible, should she decide to reveal it.

But now it was too late. She'd revealed her heart the moment his lips met hers. She wanted him again, and not as a play thing. Though she had not understood this until now, Lacy was beginning to see her future ... with Finn in it.

The fear that she had managed to skirt suddenly found her.

Finn clasped his hands in front of him and hung his head. "I'm a fool."

Her guard began to rise. "For kissing me?"

"I'm sorry," he said. "But I can't do this to my brother. He told me he was lost without you."

"Lost ... how?"

"You don't know?"

Lacy leaned her head to the side. "Finn, I have zero idea what you're talking about."

Finn's smile turned rueful. "I know he's a private guy, but I can tell when my brother is, uh, smitten."

She coughed a laugh and Finn looked stricken.

"Adrian is *not* smitten with me. He's not into me at all—I'd know it if he was. My gosh, Finn! That's crazy talk. Is that why you think he's lost without me?"

"It's not crazy, Lacy. He has said as much. Well, he said he was lost without you."

"As an employee, and frankly, I'm very honored that he would say that."

He narrowed his eyes, as if thinking. "Perhaps I misinterpreted his meaning ..."

Lacy allowed herself the freedom to laugh at that. "You definitely misheard him. Adrian and I, well, we're a good team—I'll give you that. And I hope that he really meant it when he said that I am next in line for the director position, but I think being lost without me is a stretch."

"Is that right?" Finn wore a comical smile on his face now and Lacy blushed.

"Not that I'm trying to get myself fired or anything."

"Never crossed my mind."

"I'm quite glad about that."

He grinned. "Are you now?"

She blushed again and they both turned silent, the sound of distant waves their backdrop. The tension in Finn's face had ebbed away and he reached for her glass of wine and handed it to her.

"A toast," he said. "To getting lost ... over the next two weeks."

She smiled at him, amused. "Salud."

They tapped their glasses, sipped their wine, and settled into the sound of roaring waves.

5

"I thought this was going to be a tiny wedding." Lacy stabbed Maggie's lemon cheesecake with her fork and took a bite. "I mean, party favors? Don't buy candles and burlap on my account."

Maggie slapped her hand. "They're announcements, not favors. Would you look at these, please?" She gave Lacy an exasperated little frown. "What's gotten into you anyway?"

Lacy smiled, unable to hide it. She took another bite of Maggie's cheesecake then quickly pulled her hand away to avoid another assault. "Nothin's going on with me. It's just a lovely day in the neighborhood."

"Really? This coming from the girl who had seriously no interest in coming back. Or so she said."

Lacy sat back, her body relaxed, her mind hopeful. "What can I say? I've seen old Colibri in a new light lately."

Maggie stuck her tongue to her upper lip and squared a look on her sister. "Do tell."

"Do tell ... what? We're at the beach. Can't a girl relax on her vacation?"

"Maybe. But, I don't know, you seem awfully giddy." Maggie quirked her chin, eyeing Lacy. "Did you get that promotion?"

The promotion. For the first time in months, she had forgotten all about the carrot that had been dangling in front of her, the prize that had kept her moving forward. A sweet, hot, unexpected kiss could do that to a girl. She licked her lips, smiling. "Not yet. But I will, soon."

"So you're still in talks for it."

"I am."

"Well, then, great!" Maggie plucked an announcement from the samples. "This one. I like this one. What do you think?"

Lacy peered at the sketch of a happy couple with a thought bubble over their heads. Wasn't formal, like she would choose, but considering Maggie was marrying the town's hotshot surf pro, she thought it worked for them. "It fits you. I suggest you order a million of them right now so you can move on to the next thing on your to-do list."

Maggie smiled and continued to stare at the sample announcement. Lacy had never seen her big sister quite so happy before, and though she considered a few sarcastic comments she could interject, her usually snide self was in hiding today. Nothing Maggie could say could change her mood.

"I have a favor?"

"Shoot."

"Would you be willing to take some candid shots on Saturday? Luke talked me into hiring a local photographer for professional shots, but I'd like to have some that don't look so posed."

"I'd love to. I don't have a fancy camera anymore, though."

"You've got the newest iPhone, so that would be perfect. I'll ask Daisy to take some too so you aren't burdened so much."

"Speaking of pictures, I want to show you something." Lacy took her phone from her purse and clicked on the photos icon. She found the one of Finn contemplating the deep and vibrant sky just after the sun had set last night.

"Is that Finn?"

Lacy began to say yes when she noticed Maggie looking elsewhere. She followed her sister's gaze toward the window. Finn and Lillian Madsen were walking on the sidewalk at a fast clip, like they were late for a meeting. She leaned forward, noticing how different he looked compared to last night. Though he wore a sport coat instead of a suit, Finn looked stiff, his hair in an ultra-professional smoothed-back style, unlike the waves she ran her hand through last night.

She shut her eyes, remembering all the feels that time with him had brought. Had it been a dream? A one-off? Her eyes snapped open and she drew a harsh breath and shook her head.

Maggie watched her with a certain curiosity. "I know you think I'm just your nosy big sister, but girl, you have it bad for him, don't you."

Lacy's eyes bored into Maggie's.

"It wasn't a question."

"Define bad."

"Ha! I knew it."

"Quiet down," Lacy hissed. "It's all sort of new." She turned her glance toward the window again, but Finn and Lillian had disappeared just as Rafael wandered into the bakery. She pulled her attention back to her sister.

"So why is he hanging around Lillian? She's such a pill. Did you know she marched into Luke's shop the other day and told him she had a buyer?"

"Luke's selling his shop?"

"No! She's just trying to sniff out listings. He played with her a little and asked to see the offer, even though he has no thought of selling. She wouldn't discuss it without him signing a year-long listing agreement—which he would never do." Maggie crossed her arms. "There's something wrong with that woman."

Brooke Lamont appeared at their table, a grim look on her face and a coffee pot in hand. "Lillian giving you ladies trouble again?"

Lacy's mood was quickly sinking. "It's her super power." She pushed her coffee mug over to the side of the table and watched Brooke fill it up.

"How about you?" Maggie asked. "You any closer to getting that boyfriend of yours to settle down?"

Brooke smiled, but it did not stretch as far as her eyes. "Oh we'll see, we'll see."

"Sorry if I'm being too nosy." Maggie gave Brooke a sympathetic smile.

"May I ask," Lacy said, "who is your boyfriend?"

"Oh that's right. You don't know." Maggie gestured toward the window. "Brooke's dating Lillian's son, Trent."

"No way."

Brooke grinned. "Way. And I didn't mean that there's

anything wrong, it's just"—she shrugged—"he has been traveling a lot lately, and I think we may have just hit the muddy middle."

Lacy laughed. "What does that mean?"

"Oh, you know, the middle of the story when you don't know exactly what the hero and heroine should do next to take things to the next level."

Both Lacy and Maggie stared at Brooke, wordlessly.

Brooke giggled. "My mom was a novelist."

"Makes sense," Lacy said.

Maggie slid her coffee cup over for a refill. "If I were you, I wouldn't worry about a thing. I've seen you two together and that guy's smitten."

Lacy jerked a look at her sister.

"What?"

"Nothing. It's just I haven't heard the word smitten in years, and now I've heard it twice in twenty-four hours."

Maggie slapped the table and pointed at Brooke. "See? It's a sign."

"I'll take it!" Brooke smiled, her expression visibly relieved. "Anything else I can get for you ladies?"

They assured her they'd had their fill of sugar and caffeine for the morning.

As she walked away, Rafael stopped by their table. "Mornin', ladies."

Maggie held up her coffee mug. "Hey, Rafael."

He nodded at her but fixed his gaze on Lacy. "Sorry I didn't make it over yesterday. I was tied up."

Lacy avoided Maggie's penetrating stare. No doubt her mind was lingering on Rafael's use of the term tied up and wondering what he meant ...

"I forgive you," Lacy said, hoping he'd just move on already.

"Let me make it up to you."

She shook her head. "Not necessary. I ended up having all the help I needed yesterday after all." Lacy winked at Maggie before returning her gaze to Rafael.

He gave her a long, slow look before nodding. "Enjoy your afternoon, then."

As he headed out the door, Maggie said, "He's a curious one. Still gorgeous. Mysterious."

"Flaky."

"Maybe so." Maggie shrugged. "Anyhoo, getting back to me."

Lacy laughed. "Yes, let's."

"I want you to know that you are welcome to bring Finn to the wedding."

Lacy tilted her head, scrutinizing her sister. "But you don't even know him."

"If you like him, I like him. The invitation is open."

Lacy took a sip of her coffee. "I will let you know before Saturday."

"Great." Maggie took one last drink from her coffee cup and stood. "I've got to run over to my graphics girl and get these finalized so I can write out a stack of envelopes and get them in the mail."

Lacy shrank back. "This week?"

"Absolutely! I want recipients to open them up and see that I've already married my prince."

"Gross."

Maggie chuckled. "There she is. I'd been wondering

what happened to my sarcastic sister." She brushed a kiss on Lacy's head and took off, ever the excited bride-to-be.

Lacy sat a few minutes more, her hands cupping the coffee mug as she soaked in the silence. She peeled another look out the window but Finn—and Lillian—were nowhere in view. Finn was first and foremost here to do a job—to scope out a potential site for his first coastal property. So it should not have been a surprise to her that he would meet up with that shark again.

In some ways, Lacy admired the woman. Though she was hardly likable, she did manage to obtain most, if not all, of the area's choice listings.

Admiration aside, something niggled at her, but she forced the worry away. Last night had been magical, though she wouldn't be using such fatuous language in front of any of her sisters. She had a reputation to maintain, after all.

Lacy fortified herself with a last sip of coffee and a fresh inhale. Finn hadn't said anything about seeing each other today, or any day, for that matter. But they had toasted to the next two weeks. Hopefully, they would find a way to each other before the calendar turned and she was on a plane back to Vegas.

On her way out of the bakery, Lacy waved to Brooke and hooked her beach bag over one shoulder. She had walked here, inspired by the warm day and the calm seas. Both would make for some great photos and she decided to spend the afternoon snapping shots. For old time's sake.

A few minutes later, she wandered out behind the family home to the expanse of sand. She remembered being annoyed by the long walk from the water to the house, the stickiness of wet sand that had caked in places triggering her childhood outbursts. As she recalled, Grace whined about it the most—she'd have to give her grief about that the next time they spoke.

How silly they all were to have such little appreciation for all they had been given. She sighed, watching the day's gentle waves curl toward the sand break. Plovers skittered up and down the shoreline in packs, both retreating from and chasing waves, their furry, feathered bodies rifling in the wind.

She pulled her phone from her purse, aimed, and shot bursts of photos of the birds and their antics. A throat-wrenching call announced the arrival of a gull, then another. She zoomed in and shot one, two, three photos of the menagerie that had formed. A whoop, followed by a laugh, pulled her gaze northward to where a guy and two women plunged into the waves. They reappeared, the women laughing loud enough for their voices to carry. They each grabbed one of the guy's arms and pulled, like he was their prize at the end of a game of tug o' war.

Rafael.

At least he had a very good reason to go without a shirt. Not that a warm summer day wasn't reason enough, but the guy had maintained quite the reputation since high school, showing off his tan year-round, if the reports were to be believed.

Lacy laid on her stomach in the sand like she used to as a teen. The earth felt warm and comfortable as it molded to her body—not too hot, soft and yet gritty. She propped herself on her elbows and turned her screen to landscape, taking a wide-angle view. A pelican dove. Click. A stand-up paddle boarder sought to commandeer a wave from a bevy of surfers who waited patiently. Click. Her camera picked up the three bodyboarders again. Rafael dove into a wave, as if to rescue the women, but came out flipping the water from his hair as he emerged. Click, click, click.

She laughed. He wasn't fooling anyone.

Lacy carefully put her phone in her bag, rolled herself into a sitting position, and swept off as much sand as possible. The sun had begun to grill her and her back twinged in places after the spasming episode of last night.

Reluctantly, she collected her things and headed back to the house. She carried her shoes with two fingers and tried to ignore the anticipation that was building within her. Would Finn call? Stop by? Or would he be all business today and work until the sun set and she had all but given up?

Wait, wait, wait. Get ahold of yourself, Lacy. She had never been one to wait around for a guy to call her, to put any of her own plans or thoughts on hold until he showed himself. In fact, if she wanted to, Lacy could march right up to Finn's front porch and knock on his door herself.

She cast a glance in the direction of Finn's vacation rental, a self-deprecating half smile growing on her face. Where was all this blustering coming from? Her mind flooded with her to-do list, the list unfurling, and she determined to go back home. She would pour herself a glass of wine and download her new photos. Might even find a perfect one or two to frame and put on the walls to welcome potential buyers when the time came.

Lacy had barely traipsed back into the house, the floors creaking beneath her feet, when her cellphone rang. Adrian. She sighed. Really? She didn't have to answer the call, but curiosity got to her.

"Lacy! It's so good to hear your voice."

She hesitated. He sounded too nice. "Hello, Adrian."

"Are you enjoying your time away from Las Vegas? Weather treating you well?"

She dumped her bag onto the table, frowning slightly. Surely Adrian hadn't called to talk about the weather. "I'm having a lovely time. And you?"

"Oh you know, same here—lights, glitz, desert." He laughed, the sound of it somewhat strangled.

"I can't say that I miss that too much right now." Lacy made a beeline for the fridge, opting for a cold drink on this warm afternoon. She poured herself a glass of lemonade and waited for the point of this conversation.

"Why would you? I'm sure the beach is quite beautiful."

"It is. It is." She rolled her eyes, swigged a sip, and put the glass onto the island. "Adrian?"

"Yes?"

"Is there something I can help you with?" That came out sounding testier than she would have preferred. She sucked in a breath. "I mean, what can I do for you?"

"Nothing. I called only to tell you how much I appreciate all you have done as a personal favor to me."

Oh. "Thanks." She couldn't think of anything more worthwhile to say, her conversation with Finn about this very subject—Adrian's perceived affection for her—amplifying in her head. Had she been mistaken about him? She had always worked to convey a tough shell. In business, it had served her well, kept her from becoming emotional during negotiations. Cool head, signed deal.

But sometimes that shell kept her from recognizing signs that were more personal in nature. Like right now. Was

Adrian saying that he ... that he had feelings for her that had moved beyond business?

He laughed again, his usually gruff voice unusually smooth. "I've kept you from your retreat long enough. Enjoy your next couple of weeks in Colibri. I will see you soon."

After he hung up, Lacy downed the last of the lemonade, wincing at a sudden squeeze of pain in her lower back, though she knew that her periodic issue was nothing compared to Adrian's heart condition.

No matter where she and Finn stood, she couldn't lead Adrian on to think that her acquiescence to his demands during her vacation were anything but ... professional.

FINN NOW KNEW why Lillian believed that the listing of the Holloway home was "nearly in the bag." She said the same about the Mcafee house next door, though he suspected she was crowing about that prematurely, too. But he let her go on. For one, her fantastical projections entertained him. For another, he wanted something from her as well. Walking the fine line energized him, and in the end, he suspected the outcome would be worth it.

He opened the fridge, grabbed a jug of juice and a bottle of Prosecco, and headed over to Lacy's house for an apology breakfast. Guilt seeped in and he chased it away. He hadn't phoned her yesterday. Had become too engrossed in his work, having put off answering calls and poring over contracts until after his meeting with Madsen. His projects had kept him occupied until darkness fell and he decided then to call her in the morning.

He awoke today realizing she may not have taken too kindly to being ignored, though he had not considered his behavior that way at the time.

He took the old stairs to the Holloway home two at a time and knocked on the door. Several long seconds later she greeted him, looking slightly disheveled, as if she had been roused from her bed. His heart began to careen against his chest.

"Good morning," he said.

"Morning." She yawned slightly, covering her mouth with her hand.

"I brought you breakfast."

She glanced at the makings for mimosas in his arms and laughed. A good sign.

He followed her inside, acutely aware of the effect she was having on him. Her bare feet padded along the wooden floors, the hem of her long and translucent sundress brushing against her skin. She didn't ask where he had been.

She pulled two champagne flutes from a cabinet, their glass etched from time, and stopped. "No coffee first?"

"I've already been to the bakery for espresso."

Lacy gave him a deadpan expression.

"Note to self: she's not a morning person." He quirked a smile at her. "Check."

"Mornings are a necessary evil."

He poured her drink and handed it to her. "Ah, there's where I will have to prove you wrong."

Her brown eyes peered over the top of her glass and he was mesmerized by their depth. His better judgment suggested he change the subject from explaining the way he would like to spend his mornings with her ...

"How was your meeting with Lillian yesterday?"

He faltered, but kept his expression benign. She didn't avoid saying what was on her mind, he would give her that. "Informative."

"Hm."

"What?" Finn cracked a smile.

"Have you found my description of her to be accurate?"

Finn reached for Lacy's hand and pulled her two steps closer. He reached up and looped some of her wayward hair over one of her ears. "Let's not talk about Lillian right now," he whispered.

"If that's what you'd like." She trained those big eyes on him and he found himself falling.

He leaned in for a light kiss and she didn't pull away. Another good sign. "That's what I'd like," he whispered.

Her smile engaged him.

"Let's sit outside and watch the world for a while."

"Perfect."

She led him down the hall, past several closed doors, and that's when he noticed a slight limp as she moved. As they stepped out onto the deck, he reached forward and touched her back gently. Strands of her hair caught on the breeze, tickling his face. "Are you still having pain?"

"A little. I walked a lot yesterday, which was a good thing to do, but I should have stretched more." She laughed. "I sound old, don't I?"

"Not at all. I want you to take care of yourself, though."

"You sound like Adrian."

"How so?"

"I wasn't sure if I should say anything, but he called me yesterday and sounded rather ... weird. Well, maybe that wasn't the right way to frame it." She took a sip of her mimosa, her eyes focused out to sea. "He seemed interested to hear about how my vacation was going."

Finn groaned. "That's it. I have to talk to him."

"Why?"

He toyed with telling her the truth about his past heartbreak, but would she care to know? He wasn't interested in pity, but he knew that, though his feelings for her were growing at a dizzying pace, something held him back.

"Because he's my brother and I wouldn't want anything to come between us."

"Like a woman."

"You know what I mean?"

"Honestly, I don't. This whole conversation is strange, Finn. Your brother is a good boss in many ways, and eccentric in others—I hope that's not saying too much, but that's my assessment. The idea that he has any say in my, in our, well—"

"Love life?"

A smile lit her face. Suddenly the woman with a lot to say looked shy and he reached for her, enclosing her hand in his. "I haven't told a soul this, but my fiancée cheated on me with my best friend."

She gasped.

"Don't feel sorry for me."

"She's the one I feel sorry for."

He chuckled. "I like the way you think."

Lacy dipped her chin, watching him, her gaze sympathetic. "Is this why you expressed concern about your brother's supposed interest?"

"Exactly. Although, I'd like to think that I would not have

needed to have my heart broken before I did something to hurt my brother."

"You wouldn't have."

He smiled. "Thank you for your vote of confidence."

She leaned toward him and touched his forearm briefly. "It's great that you can laugh about it now. Was it a long time ago?"

"Six months."

"Oh. Ouch." He watched her swallow that information. "Not so long. I'm really sorry that happened to you, Finn."

He shrugged, a weight off of his shoulders. He hadn't realized how much grief he'd carried until he began letting it go. "Don't be. I didn't appreciate the way it happened, but I can honestly say that I'm glad it did."

"You've turned a corner."

"And I like what I've found on the other side." He broke out in a grin and leaned over to her for a kiss. "On a sorry note, I hate to tell you this, but I have back-to-back conference calls today."

"And I've got a spa date with my sister this afternoon—if you call the local nail salon a spa. And we're doing dinner afterward."

"You deserve it."

She laughed. "I don't know about that."

"How about tomorrow?" Finn squeezed her hand. "The forecast says it will be a perfect day for the beach. No wind. We could have an old-fashioned picnic."

Her expression turned pensive and she licked her lips, her gaze suddenly elsewhere. "I can't."

"Okay." His brain scrambled to count the days she had

left in Colibri. They were ebbing away and it was beginning to annoy him. "Then—"

"Finn? Would you like to be my date to my sister's wedding?"

That was ... unexpected. He opened his mouth, still contemplating his response.

She continued. "It's tomorrow."

"You're kidding." Had she mentioned this previously?

She laughed lightly. "Theirs is a long story, but simply put, Maggie and Luke couldn't wait for a big wedding so they recently decided on a tiny one at his beach house ... and it's happening tomorrow. Maggie would love me to bring a date to round out the party."

"Oh, I understand now. I will be a seat filler."

She spat out a laugh. "What? No!" She shook her head. "I phrased it all wrong. Maybe this is too much to ask, I mean, we've only just begun getting to know one another on a, uh, personal level."

"It's not too much." Finn winked at her. "I do have a question for you, though."

She raised an eyebrow.

"Was I your first choice?"

"Yes."

"Good. Then I won't have to clock Rafael next time I see him."

"Oh my ... what!" She threw her head back, laughing. "You're hysterical. And ridiculous too. Poor Rafael."

"Poor guy nothing." He growled and kissed her lightly again, wishing for more, but knowing his desk called. "Enjoy your spa day," he whispered. "Can I call you later for the details?"

She looked him squarely in the eyes, the thrill of her gaze sending heat right through him. "You had better."

Finn could not resist Lacy another second and cupped her face in his hands, leaning in for a long, slow kiss. With reluctance, he dragged himself away, wishing for the ability to play hooky from his work for the first time in a very long time. Maybe ever.

6

———

"We shouldn't be doing this!" Maggie tasted a sliver of chocolate mousse cake, her pearlescent nails flashing under the bakery's lights. She pointed her fork at Lacy. "I better fit into my wedding dress tomorrow."

"Luke won't love you any less if you don't."

"Hey!" Maggie's eyes grew wide, accusatory. "This is where you tell me that one small slice won't hurt me."

Lacy laughed. "Sorry. I've never been a bridesmaid before."

Maggie waved that fork in Lacy's face. "Nuh-uh. You are not a bridesmaid. Grace and Bella would kill me if I chose one of you over the other—they're already annoyed at me for not having the wedding when they could come."

"Tell me about it. Both of them complained on the phone to me this week. In my opinion, Grace has nothing to say on the matter."

"That's ... right." Maggie wagged her head and muttered, "Getting married on a cruise ship ..."

Lacy sat back, enjoying her sister's freak-out. She was finally going to marry the guy she's loved for a million years. It was a huge surprise to all of her siblings, but knowing what they all do now, everyone was happy the moment had come. "Seriously, Mags, you're gorgeous and you'll look fabulous tomorrow. Are the girls excited?" Maggies's daughter, Eva, and Luke's daughter, Siena, were set to be the actual bridesmaids.

Maggie swooned and placed a hand on her heart. "They are SO cute! You won't believe it when you see them."

"For a quickie wedding, you went to a lot of trouble. Should have let me help you. I kinda plan events for a living, you know."

"You *are* helping me by being there." She took another bite of cake and let out a little *ooh*. "I'm so glad you're bringing a date!"

A woman she had seen before but never met appeared at their table with a pitcher of water. "Hello, ladies."

"Lea," Maggie said, "do you remember my sister, Lacy?"

Lea's smile faltered. "I, yes, I think maybe I do."

Lacy tried to ignore the typical response people around here seemed to have to her, though honestly, she didn't remember Lea all that much either. She held out her hand. "Nice to see you, Lea. I recognized you some, but it's been a long while."

"Yes, it has. Nice to see you as well!" Gently she swished her hair back and forth. "Maggie's my hairstylist now for life, by the way."

"Girl!" Maggie slapped the table. "Thanks to you I have a full-fledged business. I appreciate you so much!"

Lea laughed. "I'm glad you're marrying Luke and staying put. Have you gotten any bites yet on your family home?"

Lacy frowned. "The house isn't for sale."

"Oh, no?" Lea pressed her lips together and nodded. "Good news then. I could've sworn hearing that you were selling. Ms. Mcafee too. Would be an end of an era around here if that all happened."

"May I ask ... where you heard that?" Lea frowned and looked off into space. Her eyes perked. "Oh. Right. Trent's mother—the Realtor—she said something about it. She hardly ever sets foot in here—says it's too girlie for her taste. Whatever. Anyway, she's probably going to represent my aunt's property, too."

"In Colibri?" Lacy asked.

"Yeah. Actually, my grandmother owned the place and she left it to my mother and aunt. Since my mother passed, my aunt controls those decisions now. Technically, my sister and I will receive our mother's portion—if and when she decides to sell."

"You have deep roots here, then," Lacy said.

Lea nodded. "Truly, I do."

Maggie sat back. "You guys are stressing me out! C'mon, it's my wedding eve. I don't want to talk about that—that annoying woman."

Lea laughed. "I don't blame you. Hey, by the way, what time should I bring your cake to the restaurant? Brooke will be up early to frost it and she asked me to bring it to you, but I have an appointment in the afternoon. Just want to make sure I get it to you on time."

"Oh!" Maggie said, "Thanks for the reminder—"

"Tsk, tsk." Lacy shook her head. "I said you should have let me handle this."

"Fine, Ms. Know-It-All! Can you meet Lea at the restaurant after the ceremony and make sure that the cake gets set up properly?"

Lacy offered her sister a salute. "Yes, ma'am."

Maggie turned to Lea. "See what I have to put up with from my middle sister? No respect, I tell you."

Lea turned to go but stopped. "I'm jealous of you both. My sister hasn't spoken to me much in years. I love that you two are there for each other."

When she left, Maggie became misty-eyed.

Lean squinted at her. "Oh come on. Don't get like that."

"Why not?" Maggie grabbed her napkin roughly and blew her nose with it. "We were almost like that, you and I. Not to mention Grace and Bella ... and Jake."

"What are you talking about? We've never not spoken to each other."

"No, but we've been at odds. We've given each other the silent treatment at times, maybe not on purpose, but in our pursuits."

Lacy looked away briefly. She sighed. "And secrets."

"Yeah."

Maggie sounded sad and that was twelve shades of wrong on her wedding eve. Admittedly, Lacy was the least emotional of the group, but she wasn't about to let this be the focus of their conversation.

"Mags, I want you to know that I am very, very happy for you. And I'm sorry that you and Luke were apart all these years. I also believe that the best is yet to come."

Inexplicably, Maggie sobbed now. She jumped up from her chair and lunged at Lacy, bear hugging her without any regard for the scene she was making.

"I believe that for you, too!" she said into Lacy's hair.

"For heaven's sake." Lacy laughed, self-consciously as she pulled away from Maggie. "Stop crying. You cannot cry the night before your wedding!"

"Oh Lacy! I'm just so happy." She sniffled and sat back down. "I am seriously so happy you are here right now. And I meant what I said."

"What's that?"

"I hope that for you, the best is yet to come."

Lacy nodded, silently hoping for the same.

Finn unwrapped the garment bag Helene had overnighted to him. For this trip west, he had brought extremes: formal suit wear and shorts and tees. He hadn't expected to be invited to a wedding, especially not to one where impressing his date—and her family—was everything.

He suddenly felt all of sixteen, instead of thirty-nine.

The Brunello Cuccinelli linen blazer paired with Italian fit trousers would be perfect. Fine styling but lightweight for summer. He would have to give Helene a raise.

His phone rang. Adrian.

"Hello, little brother."

Hi yourself, boss."

Finn smiled at the easy way they spoke to each other when working. He only wished that same comfortable way could transfer to their personal lives. For some reason, they had each kept their lives exceedingly private. It was something they had learned from their father, who had not told them his cancer was in an advanced stage. They learned that two days before they lost him.

"To what do I owe this pleasure?"

"I was calling to follow up on my sales manager's tour of the area. Has she assisted you as I hoped?"

"She has. To be honest, I did not originally see the purpose of my coming out here, but the personal tour has made all the difference." Finn chose his words carefully. He was planning to probe more about Adrian's feelings for Lacy, if there were any. Even if there were, did it matter considering she didn't return them?

Another thought dragged him down, a hollow ache in his gut. What had Lillian been implying about Rafael and Lacy? Surely that had been nothing but rumor.

Adrian broke into his thoughts. "That's good news! Have you found a property?"

Finn blinked slowly, turning his thoughts to the moment. In reality, he was not quite ready to answer that question. He had an idea, but it was in its early stages, and more questions needed answering. Besides, he rarely revealed his plans—even to family. Maybe he was more like his brother than he once thought.

"There are possibilities," he said.

"Ah. Good. I knew Lacy could help you. She's a tough one, but she knows her stuff."

Finn chuckled.

"Of course, you were the one that spotted that about her when you recruited her right out of that trade show. I was only the lucky recipient of her charms." He paused. "Tell me about the area."

Finn stiffened. "Colibri?"

"Yes. I've noticed a change in Lacy and I'm wondering if, perhaps, the salt air has brought that on. I know you are there purely for business, but have you found other benefits from living near the sea?"

Loaded question. Finn was a through-and-through city guy. Until recently, he could not imagine life without the smell of the bustle, the cufflinks and French collars, the city lights after dark. He thought of Lacy, though, and smiled. "Yes, I have," he said. "Life is slower here."

"And you like that?" His brother sounded unconvinced.

"It's new."

Adrian laughed. "You'd tire of it, I'm sure. Shoot, if you're singing its praises, maybe I should go out there for some R & R soon."

Finn's smile dimmed. Was his brother's heart acting up again?

Adrian continued. "Seriously, though, I've been thinking about Lacy ..."

Me too, brother. Me too.

"And I think you should consider her for a property out there, should you find the right place to build. She would be the perfect person to run that resort."

Finn grew pensive. Adrian mentioned that he might like to come to California for rest sand now he's suggesting Lacy to run the new property? Was he thinking long-term about her? About them? He had to squelch these musings of his brother, carefully and quickly.

"Back up," Finn said. "Are you saying that you'd rather not turn over the Vegas property to Lacy?"

"I'm not saying that—she would make a fine director of sales and marketing. Just a minute." Finn could hear Adrian addressing someone in the background. He came back on the line. "You still there?"

"I am."

"Good. All I was saying is that you need to consider how much she knows about the West coast. She probably has more contacts out there than she does here. She certainly has the interest, based on the way she sounds whenever I've called her."

Finn sat on the fainting couch by the window. "Listen, Adrian, I want to talk to you more about Lacy—"

"I do as well, but I gotta go. A client is in the waiting area to talk about holding a massive writers conference here, a big move from their last place. I don't want him to run."

"This is important."

Silence. "Proceed."

"Adrian, do you have personal feelings for Lacy?"

"I like Lacy very much."

"I see. Have you told her how you feel?"

"What're you talking about? Has she been complaining about me? I gave her a nice review and a small raise—is she asking you for more?"

"That's not what I am referring to and I think—I believe you know that. Let me rephrase: Are you in love with Lacy?"

A long silence ensued. Then laughter, boiling over. "What—who gave you that idea? Did—wait, does Lacy have a thing for me?"

"No, nothing like that." Relief came like a puncture from

a helium balloon. Finn dropped his chin, his forehead landing in the cradle of his palm. He had been mistaken about Adrian's feelings, apparently wrong enough to send his brother into convulsive laughter.

"Phew. That's a relief!" His brother chortled, the sound of it like that cartoon rooster Foghorn Leghorn. "Not like it would be a surprise or anything. I am quite the catch you know."

"Oh I know."

"I'm sure HR will be thrilled to know that my sales manager and I are not carrying on. In all seriousness, while Lacy and I aren't involved in any way, I would have to be completely self-absorbed not to notice how men look at her." He laughed again. "Rumor has it more than one client has slipped his number into her hands."

Finn stood abruptly. "That's enough."

"You're the one who brought it up. All I'm saying is she's a looker, no doubt."

"Fine. Great. Let's move on."

"Yes, sir, boss."

"Have you suddenly become a child? Why the attitude? I asked you a simple question that required a straight answer. I am not asking for any further commentary."

"Be obedient to the boss. Got it. Anything more before I go and try to save a client for you, my liege?"

"Goodbye, Adrian."

With a click, he was gone. Finn stared at the phone. He should have been thrilled. He was, at least as far as his brother's feelings for Lacy were concerned. If he were to pursue her, he would not have to worry about doing to Adrian what Brad had done to him.

Then why the tumult in his gut? Was it simply Adrian's sorry attitude and the way they had left the call? Maybe. Finn checked the time and sighed. He'd have to get a move on if he was going to make it to the wedding on time. Lacy was already with her sister, helping with her dress. He swung a look back at the attire hanging in his closet, waiting for him. He only hoped that the clothes he wore would be enough to camouflage his current state of mind.

7

"Maggie, you're beautiful."

"You say that like you're surprised."

Lacy's mouth fell open and she frowned. "Wow. Do I really seem that mean to you?"

"No, honey. You're not mean, just opinionated."

"Like you're not."

"Maybe there's attitude in our genes." Maggie laughed. "I think I'm a little nervous."

"About what?" Lacy fussed with the folds in Maggie's dress. "For heaven's sake, you've been mooning over this boy —this man, actually—for years and now you're finally about to marry him!"

"See? That's the usual Lacy." She groaned. "It's just that everyone thinks that being the first born means I'm an extrovert, but it's so not true. I'm literally nervous about saying my vows in front of Luke's mother and Wren—oh, and Daisy and Jake." She fanned herself with a handkerchief. "This came on all of a sudden. Isn't that dumb?"

"Not really." Frankly, that kind of attention would make Lacy cringe too. "But I know you love the guy. Maybe you should be like the runaway bride and go off by yourselves on some hill with only the preacher to hear you."

Maggie clapped. "Yes! Or out to the shoreline!"

Lacy smiled, her mind suddenly carrying her to that favorite spot on the hill, the secret place that she had run to as a kid.

Maggie snapped her fingers. "Earth to Lacy. Where did your mind go? You're smiling like you've got a secret."

"Sorry." She could have lied and said she was thinking about work, but how would that look on her sister's wedding day? "I was just picturing you and Luke getting married out on the beach in bare feet." So maybe she still lied. A little.

"Ooh, but then I wouldn't get to wear these sparkly shoes!" Maggie scooped up a pair of jewel-encrusted flip-flops and dangled them from her fingers.

"Those are seriously cool." Lacy ran a finger along the sparkling jewels. "And I'm not just saying that to be nice."

"Trust me. I know!" Maggie laughed heartily now. "Aw, Lacy, thanks for being here. I'm feeling more relaxed already."

Just wait, Lacy thought.

Maggie snapped her fingers. "Oh! Don't forget about the cake. Lea promised me she would have it to the restaurant, but not until right before it's time to walk over."

"No problem. I'll meet with her and make sure everything is all set up for when you and lover boy walk through those doors."

Maggie held splayed palms against her chest. "You're my favorite sister—but if you tell the others, I'll call you a liar."

"No doubt."

In the background, they heard the doorbell ring and various shoes traipsing across the home's wooden floors. Lacy took a peek at the clock on the nightstand and realized Finn would be here soon. Or maybe he had arrived along with the others. A small tumble through her stomach told her—she had it bad for him. When was the last time her middle did a somersault at the thought of seeing a man?

Maggie stood and sashayed over to the full-length mirror leaned up against the wall. She smoothed her manicured hands down the beading of the dress, smiling.

"You done good," Lacy said, admiring the dress. "Ready to go and get hitched?"

Maggie nodded. A tiny squeal escaped her and she took Lacy's hand and squeezed it.

Lacy squeezed it back. "Listen, I'm going to check on Eva and Siena again and make sure they are in position. You still have about twenty minutes. I'll make sure your guests are here and that Luke hasn't run off to some surf competition somewhere—"

"Don't even kid about that!"

Lacy stepped out of the bedroom, laughter rolling from her. She came across Luke first. "Ready for my sister?" she quipped.

"Couldn't be more ready," he said.

"Where are the girls?"

Luke pointed to the back deck of the house where the wedding would take place. "They are outside impatiently waiting to become official."

"That's the sweetest thing I've heard today. Well, other than your fiancee going on and on about you in there."

Luke laughed. "Wish I could have listened in."

"Something tells me you'll be hearing all about it soon enough."

Luke chuckled. "Hope you're right."

Lacy gave his cheek a little slap. "I'll go check on the girls and make sure everyone is seated."

"Appreciate it. I'll check in with Zack and make sure he plays the wedding march and not something else from his playlist." Zack was a teenaged regular at Luke's surf shop and he played guitar, apparently.

"Good thinking." Lacy made her way through Luke's charming beach house and out onto the deck where guests were quietly milling about. Thankfully this deck was about ten times the size of the one at the Holloway house, big enough to hold both the wedding party and the extra guests who had joined in.

"Lacy!" Bella practically flew into her sister's embrace, a fluffy Pomeranian nestled in the crook of one arm.

Lacy held her forefinger to her mouth, fighting not to fall off her heels. "Shh!"

"Okay," Bella stage whispered, barely able to conceal her laughter. "I'm so excited to be here! Do you think Maggie suspects anything?"

"No way."

Grace flounced over, her hunky husband Chase following closely behind. "Congrats on being able to keep a secret." Grace pulled Lacy into a hug, her growing stomach wedging itself between them. When she pulled back, she held onto her sister's hands. "You look amazing, by the way."

Lacy had chosen a floral midi dress in mauve, the fabric sheer in places. She paired it with a pair of strappy heels—

the tallest ones she owned. Finn towered over her anyway, so she figured, why not?

"Thank you, Grace. You look ... healthy."

Grace cracked up. "You always did have a way with words —not."

"Hi, sis." Chase leaned down and gave Lacy a kiss on the cheek.

"Maggie's going to be so surprised you're all here. Guaranteed ..." Lacy spotted Finn as her words trailed off. She knew the moment he made his entrance onto the deck, a Greek god come to life. Thankfully, she was still holding one of Grace's hands. Kept her from swooning.

"Who in the world is that?" Grace said, craning her neck.

"He's no one, my love. Eyes up here." Chase took his wife's hand from Lacy and tucked it into his folded arm, eliciting light laughter from Grace.

Even Bella sighed a little, her voice a whisper. "He's really handsome."

Finn approached the group, no sign of timidity in him. He strode toward them, a smile on his face, his eyes covered in shades. Captivating.

When he reached her, Finn took one of Lacy's hands and kissed it. He did not let her go but turned to the others. "Hello, everyone."

"I'd like you all to meet Finn Hastings." Lacy introduced them one by one. He shook each person's hand, while still holding onto hers with his other one.

Grace pointed a wide-eyed look at Lacy that held a question in it, while Bella tilted her head to one side and stared up at Finn as if framing him in one of her art projects.

Three more people appeared in the doorway. Wren

pushed her Rollator across the deck, the sound of it like wheels on a pier. Her daughter, Daisy, helped her find a seat. And Jake, Lacy's big brother and Daisy's fiancé, hovered over the both of them. Would wonders never cease ...

She scanned the far end of the deck where Siena and Eva had been talking nonstop since Lacy had stepped outside, and they were still there, looking pretty and possibly a little bored. Everyone was here. Lacy walked up to the front of the deck where a flowered arch stood. She greeted the pastor of Colibri Church, his smile never-ending. Then she nodded to Luke who had taken his position in the waiting zone, and turned to the small group of family and friends. "Thank you all for coming. I know Maggie's going to be very touched that you all made the trip here."

Lacy's voice caught on the last few words, surprising herself. She licked her lips a moment, noting how Bella was already dabbing her eyes with a tissue. She cleared her throat. "So. Let's get this party started, shall we? I'll let the bride know we're ready."

Jake joined her on the way back into the house. "I wish Dad was here," he said.

Lacy paused in the hall. She put her hand on Jake's chest and gave him a solemn nod. "Me too." Her voice cracked.

Jake smiled. "I'm honored to be his stand in—for any and all of you."

Lacy nodded and inhaled, righting her shoulders. "Thank you." She knocked on the door, all smiles now, and peeked her head inside. "All ready to marry your dreamboat?"

Minutes later, Lacy cued Zack to start the music and took her seat next to Finn. She could almost feel Grace and Bella's eyes on her. Patience, ladies, she thought. *You know almost as much as I do about this relationship.*

Within seconds, though, everyone had turned to watch as Siena and Eva walked down the center aisle together and took their places—Eva on the bride's side and Siena on the groom's. Maggie, accompanied by Jake, stood on the threshold of her new life. Her gaze was squarely on Luke's, her smile wide, her eyes already flooded. They made it about halfway down the short aisle when she let out a wail.

"You're here! Oh my gosh, you're both here!"

Bella leaped up to hug Maggie, with Grace close behind. Jake stepped back as the three girls huddled in the narrow aisle, crying and carrying on as if they hadn't spoken in years. While that wasn't close to being true—the weekly calls had cured that—the last time they had all seen each other in person was to say goodbye to their parents.

Lacy found herself welling up again. What was happening to her? Maybe all this sea air was making her soft.

"That's a beautiful smile on your face," Finn whispered.

She felt her skin flush. Lacy hadn't realized how lost in thought she had fallen. She peered at him. "Maggie said today that she's an introvert."

Finn chuckled.

Lacy looked to see Maggie lean over and kiss Chase on the cheek. She gave Grace's barely-showing belly a pat before straightening and reaching again for Jake's arm. "I know," she said, "I'm not buying it either."

They were both still laughing quietly by the time Maggie made it to the altar, so to speak, and Jake took his seat with Daisy and Wren.

Lacy let out a relieved sigh and listened as the reverend began, "Dearly beloved ..."

LACY COULDN'T STOP SMILING. She usually prided herself on not smiling at the wrong time, such as when she was in negotiations. As a sales manager in the hotel industry she had learned to strike a balance between emotion and straight talk. Give the clients what they need and convince them they don't need what they think they do. Smile only when it could be done sincerely—clients could spot a fake one and use it as their reason to walk away.

"That was a beautiful ceremony," Finn said, breaking her concentration. He leaned in closer. "And you are stunning."

She turned, their faces inches apart. Her mind swayed with scrambled thoughts. She was supposed to do something now, wasn't she? His lips distracted her, as did his warm breath on her skin.

"Aunt Lacy?"

She blinked and turned to see Eva standing next to them. Her brown hair had grown out long and wavy, much like her mother's, her gaze expectant.

"Yes, Eva?"

"My mom said you're supposed to go to the restaurant and get the cake set up."

"That's right!" Lacy abruptly stood. She spun a look toward the door and then back to Finn who watched her with mild amusement. "What are you laughing at?"

He shrank back, a chuckle in his voice. "I didn't realize how much you enjoyed ... cake."

Lacy put a hand on her hip and he took it in his. Playfully, she tried to pull it away. "I have to walk over to the restaurant and meet Lea. She's delivering the cake right now."

Finn did not let her go but stood up. He took her other hand in his and lowered his chin. "I'll go with you."

She smiled and gave him a whatever shrug, but he laughed at her again.

They headed for the back steps when Jake approached them. He eyed Lacy like a protective father and stuck out his hand to Finn. "Jake Holloway."

Finn shook his hand. "Finn Hastings."

Lacy cut in. "I've been wanting to introduce you two. Finn is my—"

"Date." Finn smiled at her.

Lacy smiled back and then addressed her brother. "Finn owns Hastings Resorts. Listen, why don't you two stay and talk a moment while I go and set up the cake." When Finn began to protest, she put her hand on his chest. "I'll be fine."

Jake assessed her date. "I'll make sure Finn doesn't get lost on the way over, Lace."

Finn said, "If you're sure."

She nodded. "I am. See you in a few." Lacy dashed down the back steps and around the corner to the front of the house. The restaurant was a short walk away. After only a few steps she could smell the aroma of tomatoes and garlic floating on the breeze and her stomach grumbled.

The maître d' met her at the entrance. "Ah, I believe you are here to meet with the baker."

"I am." Lacy peered over him to the back of the restaurant where she spotted Lea. "I see her." Lea stood next to the most beautiful two-tiered cake topped with a plastic wavy-haired surfer and his brown-eyed bride.

"Wow." Lacy gasped as she approached. "Brooke outdid herself. Please tell her how beautiful it is."

"I agree. Did you notice the little sea stars in white?"

"Gorgeous. Too bad I can't hire you in Vegas."

Lea frowned. "Stay here and you can hire us anytime you want."

"Believe me, I've thought about it!"

"Well, I hope you think about it more." Lea lifted a stack of white plates from a crate. "How was the wedding?"

"Perfect. Quick." She laughed. "Here. Let me help."

"I brought along some cuttings from my garden. Thought they would drape nicely around the table after we set up the basics."

Lacy noted the white cabbage roses and asparagus fern. "Perfect. All of it. Actually, these remind me of another garden around here."

"The one up on the hill?"

"You—you know about that place? The old house?"

"That's the one I told you about recently. It was my grandmother's. She lived there a long while until she was too ill."

"Oh—wow. I had no idea."

"You've been up to see it, I take it?"

Lacy measured her response. She didn't want to annoy Lea with the ghost house reference. "When I was a kid, I often would wander up there. Always wondered whose it was."

"Some say it's haunted."

Lacy's mouth opened.

"It's okay." Lea laughed. "I've heard it all. My aunt isn't interested in living there—though it has nothing to do with that—but she's kept up the gardens anyway. Well, a gardener has, to some extent."

"I see. I believe you mentioned that she has shown interest in selling recently, right?"

"Not really. It was the other way around."

Lacy tilted her head, confused.

"I mean, someone has shown interest in the property." Lea continued to set up plates and silverware on the table as she spoke. "I think the main reason she hadn't pursued selling is that the house needs a ton of work. She figured she, well, *we* would have to put money into it in order to sell it and that hasn't appealed to her very much. But, I don't know, maybe if someone makes her a great offer then she'll agree."

Lacy's heart began to race. She had shown Finn the place at the top of the hill that had always felt like, at least in her childhood, her secret place. He ... couldn't. Right? Hadn't they both said it wasn't suited for a resort? Or ... wait. She wracked her brain. Maybe she had mused that it could be considered for something smaller, something ... boutique.

She bit the inside of her lip. Was ... was Finn about to make an offer on her favorite property in all of Colibri Beach? Without telling her? He certainly didn't have any obligation to divulge his real estate negotiations to her. But really?

A cluster of voices began to fill the dining room. "You'd better go," Lea whispered. "I'm about done."

"Thanks, Lea. Looks lovely."

Lea turned to see Finn and Jake still in conversation. Maybe Finn was laying out his plans to rip down the old ghost house and build some monstrosity up there. Nice of him to tell her about it first. She swallowed. Should have never exposed that part of herself to him. Probably seemed pretty dumb at the time. What was she thinking? That a billionaire hotel developer would not see the potential that she saw in that once-loved old place?

Tears pressured her eyes, but she blinked them back. Lacy had been called a lot of things—stubborn, humorless, ice queen—but not silly. At this moment, though, she felt silly and ridiculous, spoiled even. If she really wanted to stay in Colibri, she could arm-wrestle her siblings for the family home once the requirements of the will were fulfilled. Of course, she would have to find work first. And money.

Finn broke away from Jake and approached her, his smile wide. She tried to paste on a smile, but it wasn't her thing. Concern knit his brow and he steered her away from the crowd by the elbow. "You okay? Did something happen?"

She ran her tongue along the underside of her upper lip, stalling.

A familiar voice interrupted them before she could respond. "There you both are." It was Wren, holding on to her walker. "I'm so pleased that you two have become so well acquainted. Lacy, you were such a dear to bring—Mr. Johnson, is it?"

"My name is Finn," he said, kindly.

"Well, now, that's right. And such a very exotic name too!" She turned to Lacy and with a wink said, "See what happens when you do a good deed?"

Lacy looked Finn squarely in the eyes. "I do indeed."

Daisy sidled up behind her mother. "Let's find our seats, Momma. I'm starved."

"See? This is why you need to be home more—so I can feed you!" Wren touched her daughter's face gently before they made their way over to a table.

Finn rubbed her shoulder. "Lacy, if there's something bothering you, let's talk about it."

She nodded tightly, her eyes flitting about. "Yes. We need to do that, Finn. I've heard something—"

Maggie and Luke made their entrance to her sisters' cheers. Jake whistled. And Eva stood next to her sister, Siena, one arm hooked around her neck. How could Lacy's mood be so sullen in an atmosphere like this?

Finn casually turned toward her. "What have you heard?"

"Aunt Lacy!" Eva and Siena skipped toward her, oblivious to the turn in her conversation with Finn. "Take our picture," Siena said, mugging for some non-existent camera.

"Yes, ma'am," Lacy said, turning to Finn. He handed her bag to her without a word and she removed her iPhone.

The girls wrapped their arms around each other and yelled, "Cheese!"

Lacy took a burst of photos and stood back, checking the lighting on the shots as the girls ran off to who-knew-where. She flipped a look upward, catching eyes with Chase. The guy had been a lawyer a long time, much longer than Grace had. He'd been trained to watch body language, and in some ways, so had she. She could tell by his expression that he was concerned. He was telegraphing a question to her and she was ... ignoring it.

"Shall we take our seats?"

Lacy snapped a look up at Finn. Why, why, why did he have to be so handsome? So chivalrous? She exhaled, pushing away her suspicions. Maybe, just maybe, it was a coincidence that the very month she had taken Finn to see the ghost house, someone else had fallen for it as she had.

He offered her his arm and a question with the raising of his brows. "May I?"

His voice, like silk, both soothed and frightened her. She wanted to think the very best of him, but feared she couldn't. Still, Lacy slipped her arm into his and let him lead her into the dining room to join the others in celebrating the very best day of her sister, Maggie's, life.

8

S he had been avoiding this moment all night.

"Ready to leave?" Finn's smile was good-natured, though she sensed tension in his gaze. He had been nothing short of amazing all night, wowing her family with conversation both deep and friendly, never superficial or dull. More than once she'd noticed Bella mooning at him, and Grace had winked at her when she caught Lacy staring at him.

She nodded and took his hand when he offered it. It was cooler to the touch than she remembered.

Maggie approached her and hugged her neck, causing her to let go of Finn's hand. "You're the best sister ever." Her voice sounded dreamy and perhaps a little tipsy.

"I heard that," Grace said.

Maggie laughed and hugged Grace. "And you're also the best sister—and you, too!" she said, lunging for Bella. "Thank you both so much for coming all this way for my wedding. Best surprise ever! I love you all."

Luke appeared at his bride's side. "It's time for us to go, Mrs. Hunter."

"Whoo!" Maggie lifted her bouquet into the air. "Did y'all hear that?"

"We heard it, Mags," Jake said.

"Wait—wait!" Maggie stopped Luke and turned to Bella and Lacy. "You two need to fight for my bouquet."

Lacy rolled her eyes. "Here." She plucked the flowers from Maggie's hand and gave them to Bella. "These are for you. Go find Mr. Wonderful."

Bella's signature ripply sigh filled the air. "Aw, thank you, Lacy."

Lacy clapped her hands like she was calling a team meeting. "Chase and Grace, the master bedroom is ready for you when you get to the house. Bella, you and I—and that animal of yours—will be bunking in the whale room."

"What about us?" Maggie said, her smile sly.

"You two have a honeymoon to get started—get out."

Luke took that opportunity to gently guide his bride out of the restaurant, the two of them waving and laughing the entire way.

"What about Eva and Siena?" Grace asked.

Chase cut in, "I believe I heard that they will be staying with their grandmother."

"That's so sweet," Bella said.

"And I'll camp out with Daisy and Wren tonight," Jake quipped.

Grace laughed. "Okay then. Now that everyone is accounted for, I am ready for some rest because we fly out first thing in the morning to meet with out-of-state clients. Will we see you back at the house, Finn?"

"I'm afraid not." He scanned the group. "It was a pleasure to meet you all, but I have an early morning call tomorrow as well."

Bella frowned. "Even on a Sunday?"

"Unfortunately, yes. I know you all have more catching up to do, but"—he turned to Lacy, something pleading in his eyes—"I hope you will allow me to borrow your sister for a little while longer this evening."

Grace chuckled. "Borrow away. Lacy, we'll see you in the morning."

Lacy watched as the last of her family members straggled out of the restaurant. The din of clanking plates and silverware being cleared away filled the silence between her and Finn. He led her out of the restaurant, her mind and body spent. It had been a beautiful day. Truly. But her conversation with Lea had finely sharpened the otherwise-smooth edges of the day.

"Let's walk home," she said.

"Why not?" Finn didn't skip a beat. Even though he had driven them there in his shiny rental convertible. He began down the sidewalk in the direction of their houses.

"On the beach," she said, removing her heels.

He eyed her and she thought he was about to protest. Instead, he removed his leather derby shoes, tied the laces together, and swung them over his shoulder like a pair of cleats.

The sand felt cool and soft between her toes, like a gentle loofah. She allowed herself to breathe in the night air, thankful for a clear sky to guide them home.

Finally, she broke the silence. "You asked Lillian to show you the ghost house property. Didn't you?"

"You showed me that property, Lacy."

She breathed in deeply and looked out to sea, the waves lined with silvery foam. Evading the question. Lovely.

"But, if you are asking whether I looked into it further with Lillian, the answer is yes." He paused, giving her more time to reload. "Are you not on board with me delving into the availability of this property?"

Once again, her feelings had been ignored. It rankled her. "No, I am not on board, Finn. That place was special to me and I never intended for you to—"

"Investigate it further?"

"Take the devil incarnate to my sacred place." She paused. "Did you tell Lillian how you knew about it? Why it was so special to me?"

"Of course not." His voice sounded terse.

"But you took her up there, to build your dream resort."

He didn't answer her.

"I see."

"My intent was not to hurt you—quite the opposite." Concern flitted across Finn's features. She felt certain he had more to say, but he broke eye contact with her and took a step back. Finally, he said, "I am doing my due diligence. It is always best, in my opinion, to consider all options presented."

She knew this. Deep down, she did. But it unnerved her anyway, which brought on feelings of silliness again. And that irked her more.

"Is it possible that some of what you're feeling has to do with all you and your family has endured in the past year?" His voice turned kind and she felt herself blinking away tears again. "I've had to wonder what they had been thinking with such requirements."

"What do you know about my parents? They were—they were good people!" Conflict filled her, as did fits of anger. Her mother had been ill. Her father hadn't said a thing! The tears wouldn't hold back now and she bit back a swear. This is not how she expected to spend the end of an otherwise perfect day.

Finn reached for her, attempting to hold her hands, but she resisted. "I'm sorry. I didn't mean any disrespect. When Lillian told me about their will—"

"When Lillian told you?" Lacy stopped walking. She dug a fist into her waist. "You mean, that night at the house ... when I told you about my parents, you already knew?"

He turned stone quiet. She was getting tired of seeing his stiff upper lip. Hadn't hidden emotions launched her family into turmoil? She needed truth in her life. Transparency. Not secrets and half-truths. And certainly not the sense that her feelings—and wishes—were being ignored. She'd had enough of that for a lifetime.

"Lillian mentioned it, yes."

"And what else did Lillian mention regarding me? Regarding my family? Any other little rumors out there I should know about?"

"Nothing tawdry. If I had heard anything like that, I would have shut her down." He paused. "I believe the only reason she told me about your parents' will was because she is hoping to obtain the listing for the family home when you are all ready to sell."

"Fat chance we would let her have it." Lacy spat out the words, her chest rising and falling in the aftermath. "Why would she think you cared about that anyway? You looking to buy a beach house?"

"For the resort."

"That makes zero sense."

"Lillian says she has spoken to Wren Mcafee about selling her house when she is ready to move to an assisted-living facility. She proposed that we buy several beachfront homes, seek a zoning variance, and build our resort on the sand."

Lacy recoiled. "Why didn't you tell me any of this? You-you came to my home. We drank wine. We—well, you know what we did. We could have talked all this out and I would have set you straight about Lillian and her, her fantasies. In fact, didn't I do that?" She folded her arms in front of her chest. "Instead, you pretended you knew nothing about my parents' will when all along you were planning to swoop in and buy up anything Lillian Madsen deemed unworthy to stand."

"That's far, far from true." Finn's eyes darkened. "You make me sound deceptive."

She lifted her chin. "You make yourself sound deceptive." Lacy shook her head and began walking again, faster this time, her only goal to get home soon. How she wished she had not suggested this walk and had taken his car instead.

"And what about Rafael?"

She stopped and pivoted. "What about him?"

"You told me there was nothing between you, but there's a rumor that you and he have a past. Maybe even a ... present. I suppose Lillian made that up too?" He paused and she could hear him inhaling roughly. "I saw him walk out of the bakery the other day when you were there."

"Ha. For a billionaire, you sure are so gullible!" Could this night get any worse? Anymore ... high school? She looked straight at him. "You could have said hello and cleared up your questions in two seconds."

"I'm careful. Very, very careful. But I hear you and maybe you're right." He raked his hair with a hand. "You and Maggie looked too engrossed in your conversation, by the way."

"Got it. I understand. Protect yourself at all costs—protect Hastings Resorts at all costs." She shrugged. "Some people choose money over love."

"That's not fair."

"Neither is the truth sometimes. Say what you want about Rafael, but he's been a friend to this family since we were all kids. May be a little flaky at times, but he's a catch, though no one I know has ever been able to rope him in. You asked me once about him and I told you the truth." She blew out a breath and gave him a fairly level glare. "Jealousy isn't a good look on you."

Finn bit his lip, his expression faltering, his Adam's apple bobbing as he considered her. Finally, he said, "This is crazy. Listen to me, Lacy. I'm here now. With you. Doesn't that tell you something?"

"It tells me that my character meter needs adjusting. I'm beginning to suspect that the reason you agreed to come with me today had more to do with our property and convincing us to side with Hastings Resorts when the time came to rezone this whole area."

He scoffed. "You have to be kidding. You are, right?"

Lacy shut her eyes tightly, wishing away this conversation. But really, what did she know about Finn other than he was rich, smart, and her boss? The thought tugged on her heart like fish on a line. He liked her. He had a caring side. She had witnessed those sides of him, and yet, she couldn't find it in herself to trust him.

Just like every man she cared for who had come before him. Trust was hard won in her—and he had failed to earn hers. That was the bottom line.

She opened her eyes to find him staring back at her, his expression a mix of confusion and offense. "I don't want to hurt you."

"Lacy ..."

"But I just really, really need to be alone."

He dipped his hands to his sides and nodded. For the next few minutes, they walked home. In silence.

SEABISCUIT, Bella's dog, skidded to the front door, barking his greeting. Lacy dropped to the ground, uncharacteristically in need of a hug from a dog. She scooped the mongrel up, kicked off her sandals, and melted into the living room couch.

Chase wandered into view. "I came down to catch the criminal who was trying to break in." He bent down and gave Seabiscuit a quick pet. "Scoundrel."

Lacy peered up at him. "Grace sleeping?"

"Yeah. She's more tired these days. Sleeping for two, they say."

"Best to do that while she can," Lacy said, glad not to have to divulge anything personal at the moment. "Is Bella asleep too?"

"I don't believe so. I heard the shower on down the hall."

"Ah."

Chase sat across from her for a few moments before glancing around. "You've done a nice job rearranging the house. Between you, Jake, and Maggie, this place has improved."

"Really? It's hard for me to tell. To be honest, I had forgotten what it looked like around here. I remembered the table and the map"—she glanced down—"and this ratty old couch, but that is the bulk of it."

He smiled. "Not the whale comforter?"

"Right." She nodded. "How could I forget that fat whale that we all fought over?"

"Indeed."

Lacy laughed, sincerely. Leave it to a lawyer throwing around an *indeed* to cheer her up.

"Lots of good memories of this place," Chase said.

"For you?"

"Yes. Fell in love with your sister here, you know." He glanced around. "This place was part of that—will always be. Despite your brother's stalker-like behavior."

She swallowed back the natural sarcasm that arose in her throat. Jake liked to tell the story, ad nauseam, of hiding out in this place, only to discover Grace and Chase's secret.

It would be hilarious to relive if she didn't feel so ... dreadful.

Chase slapped his lap with his hands and stood, yawning. "I'm going to head up now that I know Seabiscuit has everything under control." He began to walk away then stopped. "You okay, Lacy?"

No. No, she wasn't. Instead, she nodded and cracked a smile, albeit a small one. "I'm good. Thank you."

She listened to the creaking of the floorboards as Chase wandered down the hall to the back stairway. Soon after, the bathroom's vintage door handle squeaked followed by the sound of footfalls much softer than Chase's. Bella peeked out from the hallway, a white terry robe wrapped around her body, a bright pink towel on her head. She must have brought her own towels ...

Seabiscuit shot up in alert, spotted his mistress, let out a yap, and sprang from her lap. *Ingrate.*

"Hey, boy." Bella scooped up her dog, nuzzling her freshly washed face in the animal's fur. She plopped onto the couch next to Lacy.

"I kinda thought you would be coming home a lot later," she said.

Lacy shrugged and faked a yawn, covering her mouth in dramatic fashion. "Maggie's super-laid-back, casual wedding was actually exhausting."

"Aw. Thanks so much for all you did for Maggie. She was so surprised."

"Agreed." Listlessly, Lacy petted Seabiscuit.

"Finn is so handsome, Lacy. How long have you been dating him?"

"About three weeks."

"Shut up!" Bella laughed. "No, seriously. You always seemed so distracted on our phone calls. Was it because of him?"

"I'm being perfectly honest with you, Bella." Lacy did not want to think about Finn. In fact, part of her wanted to run into the bedroom and throw herself onto that old whale bedspread and, well, wail.

She took in a breath and told Bella how Finn ended up here. She mentioned that he was renting the place next door and that she had toured him around Colibri more than once. She left off the part about how she took him to her sacred space and he tore her heart out by trying to buy it without telling her.

"That's a lot of stuff happening in one week when you're supposed to be working on the house, too."

"My other boss asked me to, so what could I say?"

Bella pressed her lips together and watched her, as if trying to formulate a question.

"What, Bella? Just say it."

She gave a little shrug. "Nothing. I'm confused about you two. I mean, how did he go from bossman to boyfriend so quickly?"

Lacy's mind ran backward, to the night Finn stopped by and found her flat on the floor. There had been signs before then that they were growing closer, of course, but that night, everything between them seemed to change. She slid a look to her sister. "I think he was as surprised it happened as I've been."

"That's sweet, but, honey, you seem unhappy. Is everything okay with you two?"

"No. Not really."

She nodded, solemnly. "I suspected."

"And I'm not in the mood to be coy about it."

"What did he do to you anyway?"

Lacy shut her eyes again, as if doing so would help somehow. She growled, shook her head, and stood up.

Seabiscuit growled too and tried to lunge forward, but Bella held him back. "Cool it, sugar." She looked at Lacy. "Let's go cuddle up and you can tell me all about it."

Lacy snickered. "We're not twelve-year-olds, kiddo."

"Yeah, but we can pretend." Bella led the way, carrying her pet in her arms. "I forgot to tell you, I already have wine coolers in there."

"You ... what?"

"You'll love them, Lacy. They're all natural and you can have your own bottle. Come try."

Minutes later, Lacy and Bella were curled up on the big old bed with Seabiscuit lodged between them. Bella shook out her hair and crimped it with her fingers. Then she laid her towel across her pillow.

Bella took a sip of her rosé wine cooler. "Remember how we would sneak food in here sometimes late at night?"

"Vaguely."

"Well, I do. I'd sneak out of the tiny bedroom next door and scramble in here. Mom always said we shouldn't eat too late at night—"

"We'd get a tummy ache."

Bella shot a wide-eyed smile at Lacy. "You do remember."

"A lot has been coming back to me this month. Things I never knew that I didn't remember." She cast a dubious look at the small, screw-top bottle of the pink wine in her hand, but gave it a sip anyway.

"Well, I remember lots of stuff about you."

Lacy froze, bottle in hand. "Like what?"

"Like the way you always knew about the latest hair products and makeup styles. Kinda always thought you might want to be a hairstylist or makeup artist."

"You're kidding."

Bella gave Lacy a wide-eyed look, surprise in her features. "Why would I kid you about that? You were always telling Maggie about stuff you were reading in magazines."

"She never listened."

"She just acted like it. I think she was listening the whole time, in fact, I know she was because she would beg Momma to buy her some of the stuff you told her about."

Lacy squinted, thinking back. She nodded. "Like body glitter."

Bella giggled. "Yes! Like body glitter ... Daddy got so mad whenever he'd see all those sparkles in the bathroom."

"Ha! Yes." She had forgotten about that.

"Oh, and remember those fishtail braids you were obsessed about? Maggie finally learned to make them so you would stop bugging her."

Lacy groaned and put a hand to her face. "I can picture the little butterfly clips I made her put all over them after she was done."

"Oh my gosh." Bella's giggles practically foamed over.

"Sshh!" Lacy said, laughing and putting a finger to her own mouth. "You'll wake the preggo one upstairs."

Bella took another sip from her bottle of wine, a winsome smile on her face. "I've missed this."

"Yeah?"

"I always looked up to you."

"Shush. You did not."

"Uh-huh, it's true." She shrugged. "You never needed anybody to tell you what to do or to think. If you were annoyed, you'd just get on your bike and pedal away. I was always too scared to do that, but I admired you for it anyway."

Lacy leaned against the headboard and took another long sip of the wine, hoping the sugar wouldn't go to her head. "I had no idea."

"I thought maybe you didn't so I'm telling you now."

"I'm sorry you were scared. I should have taken you with me."

"I would have loved that."

Lacy cast a look at her sister, whose eyes were beginning to droop. "Thanks for telling me all this, Bella."

Her sister both nodded and yawned at the same time. Gently, Lacy took the half-empty bottle of wine from her hands and leaned across her, placing it on the nightstand. She stared at her sister for a beat then hastily kissed her on the cheek. "Night," she said.

Bella settled into her pillow, her damp hair sprawled out on it, her eyes closed. "Night, Lacy. Love you."

"Love you, too, kid." Lacy wriggled down beneath the sheets, thankful for the sudden, unexpected comforts of home that just might help her unravel the tangle of thoughts that vexed her.

THE NEXT MORNING, Finn stared into the mirror, bracing his arms on the counter, the circles beneath his eyes unbecoming. He had not slept all night, and for most of it, wondered what he had been thinking these past few weeks. Did he really believe that falling for one of his employees was advisable? Especially one with such close ties to a potential resort project?

"You ought to have your head examined," he muttered. Then he cursed. And groaned. "Why must you always speak to yourself out loud?"

He pushed away from the counter and picked up his phone to text Helene, asking her to send his pilot out to California as soon as possible. He had seen all that needed seeing. Finn rubbed his palm across his unshaven face and sucked in a breath. Telling Lacy what Lillian had divulged about her was a major faux pas on his part. He had slipped, a sure sign that the beautiful brunette had worked her way into the recesses of his heart.

Maybe he should not have let that happen. The last time a woman got to him like this ... he dropped his gaze to the ground, his breathing distinct, laboring. Paige had gotten to him. Had made herself at home in his heart—and then she'd torn it clear out of his chest.

Finn blew out a breath. He flopped his suitcase open on the bed and began packing up, taking less care than usual. He would not be needing beachwear anytime soon. Besides, it all needed to be cleaned and pressed anyway. His phone rang and he checked the screen. Helene. Perfect.

"Mr. Hastings, I'm relieved you answered."

"I take it you have contacted my flight crew?"

"No, sir. Not yet."

He slammed a semi-folded shirt into the suitcase. "The reason for this call then?" His voice sounded testy, even to him.

"It's your brother. The other Mr. Hastings."

He stopped. "Adrian?"

"Yes, sir. I received word from Drew in the Las Vegas executive office that he was admitted to the hospital for observation this morning. I called you the minute I heard and wondered—"

"If I'd like to fly to Vegas instead? Yes. The answer is yes."

"I'll take care of it, sir."

"Thank you. Text me the phone number of the hospital, too."

"Certainly."

He hung up and dialed his brother, hoping Adrian had brought his phone with him and would be able to answer it. Calling the hospital was Plan B. His call went to voicemail so he hung up and punched in the number Helene had texted to him.

"Valley Hospital."

"This is Finn Hastings. I would like to speak to a patient who has been admitted. His name is Adrian Hastings."

"One moment, sir."

The call rang for almost a minute. "Nurse's station."

He repeated his request to speak to his brother.

"I'm sorry, sir, but he is out of his room right now to undergo tests."

"May I have an update?"

"Hm. Yes. He may have had a mild heart attack. We have administered oxygen and the doctor is considering options while waiting for results of testing. If you would like to speak to him, please try back in about an hour or so."

He hung up and a new text appeared on his phone:

~

Flight delayed. Lightning storm on the east coast. Urgency communicated. Will alert you with arrival details when they are available.

"Great." He dropped his phone onto the bed and stalked across the room, leaning his arms onto the window frame. Outside, the sun burned. Beachgoers moseyed by as if his life hadn't been upended in the past twenty-four hours. His mind wandered and he frowned. Lacy. If only he could call her right now. Tell her about Adrian's relapse.

What was he thinking? She made it quite clear last night that she didn't care to speak to him. Maybe he should take that as a warning sign.

Well. He couldn't stay here while he waited. Especially knowing she—and several family members—were right next door. Finn drew in another harsh breath, grabbed his keys, and darted outside. He hopped into the rental car and drove—to where he wasn't yet sure.

Minutes later, Finn found his way to the narrow driveway that he had almost missed the past two times he had come upon it. He put his car in a lower gear and made the climb. As he crested the top of the hill, the ghost house came into view. He smiled involuntarily at the moniker he had given the place after Lacy's revelations about it.

He parked, not sure exactly why he had come here—other than the obvious. Lacy had been right. He had been contemplating plans for this property, should it be available for consideration.

Finn ran a hand roughly through his hair, feeling the

crunch of gravel beneath his shoes as he traversed the property. In some ways, he regretted coming up here with Lillian. Not that he thought as poorly of her as the town seemed to —her shark-like reputation was mild compared to what he had witnessed over the last twenty years as he built his empire. But he wished ... well, he wished that his memory of the last time he had been here had been with Lacy.

Not that it would matter now anyway.

A flurry of something caught Finn's attention. A commotion of birds flapped their wings simultaneously near the end of the lot, the cliff where Lacy had shown him the tree with her initials carved into it. His mouth twisted. Surely a woman as beautiful as Lacy would have been sought after more than she indicated she was. He'd seen her photograph as a teen and she had not been an ugly duckling. Not by any means.

He found a rock and made himself comfortable. To contemplate. Truthfully, he was angry at himself. His last call with Adrian had turned unpleasant, the exact opposite of what he had been going for that day. His brother had been somewhat of a mystery to him over the years, though he had tried to make up for their relationship shortcomings in myriad ways. His job, for instance.

Not that he would ever say as much. The last thing his brother needed was to hear that Finn considered him a charity case. Mainly because it wasn't true. Adrian did an excellent job, proving himself as a formidable sales and marketing professional early on in the development of Hastings Resorts. The problem was and is—his health. Thankfully, their mother was well and active in her older years, but the loss of their father had been a blow to all three of them.

He couldn't bear the thought of losing either one of them prematurely.

Finn felt his hip, making sure his phone was close, and tried to relax. "Better clear your mind before you lose it, Hastings."

"Do those admonishments help?"

Finn jerked his chin to the side at the sound of Lacy's voice. She held her phone in landscape mode, as if she were poised to take a photo of the expansive view. The warning sign he'd heard in his head earlier shrank to a whisper.

"Heard that, did you?"

She looked at him for a beat before looking off into the distance. "I've noticed you talking to yourself on occasion."

"A habit I picked up as a kid and never outgrew."

"We all have those, I suppose."

Finn's phone rang and abruptly he stood. "Excuse me." He answered the call, striding toward the porch of the old house.

"Finn, it's Adrian. I'm not dead."

He exhaled. "I am very glad to hear it. What are your symptoms?"

"Racing heart. Sour stomach. They're checking my enzymes and some other things, but there is no imminent sign of a heart attack, I'm told."

"Beautiful."

"I'll be back to work tomorrow."

Finn shook his head. "Hold on, Adrian. I think we need to have a long talk about this—it's long overdue."

Adrian sputtered. "I'm fine. I already told you more than I was comfortable divulging, but that should have satisfied you."

That familiar edge to Adrian's voice had returned. This time, though, Finn wouldn't stand for it. If he were speaking to any other employee, he would have put a stop to the evasiveness long ago.

"Don't tell me what should satisfy me, Adrian." He licked his teeth. "Your health is of utmost importance. Much more than the resort."

"And yet that's the first thing you try to take away from me whenever I have a small setback."

Finn raked his hand roughly through his hair. He cast a glance over his shoulder. Lacy was still at the edge of the property. She stood there, peering at her phone, as if examining a photograph.

"You indicated more than a year ago that you were ready to step aside, to take care of yourself and enjoy the freedom of retirement." Finn spoke in a hushed tone. "I sent you Lacy."

Adrian swore. "And I sent her back."

"Excuse me?"

"Why do you think I set you up to meet her in that old beach town?"

Finn darted a glance at Lacy, who still seemed preoccupied. "I still have no idea what you're talking about. Unless ... you were trying to get rid of her?"

Adrian laughed. "Bingo. For a billionaire, you can be so dense."

If he weren't his brother ...

"She stresses me out. There. I said it." Adrian spoke freely, as if meds had overtaken his mouth. "Lacy Holloway is annoying. Always has a million wild ideas about the resort, and even when I shut her down she won't take no for an answer. She would be better off spearheading a new resort out West."

Finn cracked a smile.

Adrian continued. "She's cutthroat and ... well, she's bad for my health."

A million tiny violins began to play in Finn's head and he had to force himself not to throw his head back and laugh derisively to the heavens. His brother was in the hospital—with Lacy nowhere in sight—but somehow his illness was all *her* fault?

Finn frowned. "Are you saying you sent me out here on false pretenses?"

"I hoped you'd see what I see."

Finn's temper flared. He had been trying to get rid of Lacy? "Take hold, man. Take hold," he muttered.

"What was that?" Adrian interrupted.

Finn swallowed. "I'm ordering you on a sabbatical. Starting now."

"You can't do that."

Silence. Of course, he could. Adrian just never thought he would. He held his ground, the tension growing with each tick of silence between them. Finn slid another look toward Lacy again and saw ... nothing. He whipped a look around, the phone still jammed against his head. He could see the top of her ponytail as she made her way down the steep driveway.

He swallowed. "I have to go now, but I meant what I said. You are officially on sabbatical until ... further notice."

"But what about the resort?!"

"Stay calm, little brother. I've got it all under control." He clicked off the line and jogged toward the edge of the road. "Lacy?"

She turned around, her expression unreadable.

"Sorry about the interruption. That was Adrian."

She frowned.

He shifted. "I guess you haven't heard."

"Heard?"

"He had to take a trip to the hospital."

Her expression didn't change. Still very serious, but she began to hike back up the hill. She reached him, her lips slightly downturned. He fought off the urge to kiss them into a smile. Funny how she could change his mind about anything and everything so quickly.

"Finn, is it Adrian's heart?"

"There seems to be a connection."

"I'm sorry. Is he going to be okay?"

"Yes. I believe so. Thankfully."

She exhaled.

"But I've made the decision to force him out on sabbatical."

She nodded. "Perhaps the time away will be good for him, will give him time to see his health restored fully. He's, uh, well, he can be quite high-strung at times."

"You've noticed."

She shrugged. "Hard to miss."

Finn took a step toward her. "I know you have been waiting a long while to take over his position. And I don't mind telling you, if and when Adrian is feeling well enough to return to work, it won't be as Director of Sales and Marketing." He paused. "I'd like to offer that to you, Lacy."

She tilted her chin up, those lashes of hers framing

gorgeous eyes. He wanted to say so much more, to tell her how these past few weeks had changed him, had brought him happiness he hadn't experienced in a very long time. If ever. But his heart wrestled with his tongue. So unlike him. He had never felt this way with Paige, and for the first time, he realized that his ex-best friend had actually done him a favor.

"Thank you for the offer, Finn. I appreciate that, especially during this difficult time."

Her tone was measured, even. She spoke to him like a colleague and nothing more.

"But I will have to decline." Her expression continued in its unreadable state. "I have decided to give my notice."

"Lacy, no."

"I'm leaving Hastings Resorts. Effective immediately."

9

———

She had been up since dawn, the slam of a car door followed by the whir of an engine drawing her out of an already fitful night's sleep. One look out the southern-facing window confirmed what she already suspected: Finn had left Colibri.

Lacy knelt beside the bookcase of knickknacks and old magazines in her parents' bedroom. She had already pulled out a huge stack of *Entertainment Weekly* from the 70s and another of *Highlights for Children* covering more than a decade and dusted them all off with a rag.

She had hoped that throwing herself into the work of the house, the thinning of old memories, the dusting of hidden spaces, would help her feel better somehow. She waited for relief to come, but it proved itself elusive.

Seabiscuit snuffled about, distracting her. She'd never wanted an animal in her life, the thought of having a constant furry companion underfoot less than appealing.

But maybe she had been wrong about that. The dog put his front two paws on Lacy's quads and sniffed her face. Seabiscuit sneezed, spraying Lacy with who-knew-what.

"You think you're funny, don't you?" Lacy said, peering back at the dog's marble-like eyes. "Now I need a shower, buddy."

The dog collapsed onto her lap, making it nearly impossible for her to continue. She rested her hand on the little guy and sighed. Bella had decided to stick around for a few days after the others had left and Lacy welcomed the company, for once.

"Hi, Lacy."

"Hey." Bella's appearance in the doorway drew Seabiscuit away in a hurry, Lacy's knees suddenly cold.

"I'm going to make some breakfast. Hungry?"

"Well, I don't know. Are you going to make something edible or will breakfast consist of a radish sprinkled with CBD oil?"

Bella scooped up her dog and momentarily buried her face in the dog's fur. "What're we going to do with Lacy, hmm, Seabiscuit? She is so ornery sometimes."

"I am never ornery. I just like my breakfast to be, you know, edible. And real food."

Bella giggled. "I went to the store yesterday and just you wait. I'm going to make you a tofu scramble that will make your stomach grumble."

"I hope that's all it makes my stomach do," she muttered, but it was too late. Bella, with Seabiscuit clacking along behind her, was already descending the stairs.

Alone again, Lacy began shoving stacks of magazines

into bags. One by one, she hauled them downstairs to the recycle bin in the garage, hoping her back would tolerate each trip. By the time she was done, the aroma of sautéed onion greeted her.

"Wash up, you. Breakfast is ready."

Dutifully, Lacy did as she was told, secretly hating to admit how really good Bella's cooking smelled. She took a seat at the counter, but Bella, who was holding two plates, shook her head. "I thought we could eat at the dining table, for old times' sake. I've already set us up."

Lacy followed her over to the table with its years of scars and took a seat. Bella set a colorful plate of food in front of her. "It's gorgeous," Lacy said.

"Coming from you, that's a high compliment!"

"What does that mean—coming from me?"

Bella shrugged a little, her eyes slightly hooded. "You can be a little over-honest sometimes."

"Either a person is honest or they're not."

"All I meant is that you sometimes tell me the truth when I don't really care to know."

"Oh."

Bella giggled. "That's the most honest I think I've ever been with you."

"Well, then. Congratulations, Bella-boo."

Bella wrinkled her nose. "That nickname always made me sound like an accident."

Lacy laughed for the first time since she'd quit her job yesterday, a fact she had not yet made known. "You, my dear, were no accident." She took another bite of breakfast and washed it down with a glass of juice. "I remember Mom carrying on about how you were her little blessing number five."

"Ah, that's so sweet." Bella forked a bite of the colorful tofu and vegetables, her chin turned toward the old map on the wall. "We traveled so many places, didn't we?"

Lacy nodded. The map marked all of those places and had been a fun distraction when they were kids. She always thought her mother was brilliant for hanging it there as a way to keep her motley group of children from arguing during dinner. She could hear her mother's voice in her head. Whenever a fight looked like it might erupt, she'd say, *Children, who can show me where New York City is?* Or Denver. Or Nashville. Didn't matter what locale she uttered—it always did the trick, which was, to stop the chaos.

Now, as Bella and Lacy ate breakfast, the sun pouring in through the windows, the quiet dining room unnerved her.

"You haven't said anything about Finn this morning," Bella said.

"That's because there's nothing to say." Lacy sat back, taking a break. She fiddled with her napkin. "As far as I know, he is back in Las Vegas now."

Bella dipped her chin in sympathy. A knock on the door startled them both.

"I'll get it." Lacy dropped her napkin on her chair.

Wren stood on the porch, leaning on her cane. "I hope I haven't bothered you ladies this morning."

"Not at all." She unlatched the screen door and held it open for Wren, who hobbled inside.

"Thank you, dear. I decided to try walking with only my cane and it took me a little longer than I had hoped."

Seabiscuit scampered over, snuffling around Wren's feet.

Lacy picked him up quickly, not wanting him to trip their neighbor.

"Would you like to join us in the dining room? We're just finishing breakfast."

"That would be lovely."

Bella hopped up. "Can I get you a plate?"

"Oh no, no. But I would love some water."

Wren took a seat and Bella delivered a glass full of ice water to her. A silent glance passed between Bella and Lacy right before they took their own seats.

"To what do we owe this pleasure, Wren?"

The old woman sipped her water, her hand shaking slightly, her eyes downcast. Lacy gently helped her put the water glass back on the table.

"I have an apology to make to you, Lacy."

"To me? I can't imagine anything that you would need to apologize for."

Wren sighed. "It has to do with that handsome man you are dating. I-I hope that my decision will not cause you any trouble."

"Decision?"

"Not to sell my home."

Bella swiveled a wide-eyed, questioning gaze at Lacy.

Lacy let out a scoff. She reached for Wren's hand, her skin nearly translucent, and laid her own fingers upon it. "I heard about Lillian Madsen's plans. Is that what you are referring to?"

Wren nodded.

"She was way out of line suggesting that your home—and ours—would be available anytime soon."

Bella frowned.

Lacy continued. "I told Finn as much. So don't you worry one more second about any of that. He understands completely!" She squeezed Wren's hand briefly and sat back.

Wren clasped her hands in front of her. "That is such a relief to hear. You know, I have always loved your family—"

"And soon you will be officially one of us!" Bella said this in reference to Daisy's upcoming wedding to Jake. "I only wish our parents could be here to witness all of this love."

Lacy pressed her lips together, so many emotions vying for her head and heart. She swallowed back the darkness and changed the subject. "Bella and I were just talking about the map that our parents put up many years ago. It's one of the few things I haven't removed from the walls."

Wren turned to look up it, her expression pure delight. She swung her gaze back to them. "I remember it well. You know, sometimes your mother and I would sit here and talk for hours. I would bring a pie and she would make a pot of coffee. Those are some of my fondest memories."

Bella said, "Oh I remember your pies, too, Wren. So delicious."

"Thank you, dear." Wren's eyes turned toward the map again, her gaze thoughtful. "You know, as I remember, your mother made some kind of display behind that old map up there. I can't remember exactly what it was."

Lacy tilted her head to the side. "Really? Behind the map?" She looked at Bella. "I've thought about taking that old thing down, but frankly, I was afraid to find out how dingy the walls might look once I did. Plus, it has so many memories attached to it."

"You old softie," Bella said.

"Not like me, I know." She sighed. "Well, shall we take a look?"

"Let's look!" Bella nodded. "Don't worry. I'll help you repaint or clean the wall!"

Lacy shrugged. "Fine."

Bella squealed a little, as if they were about to discover long-lost treasure. Lacy wasn't so sure. She touched the frame, her fingers landing on dust. "For heaven's sake." Bella handed her a napkin and she wiped down the edges of the frame, all the way around. Carefully, she lifted the massive map from the wall.

Bella jumped up to help when it began to wobble. "I wonder where Momma and Daddy found this thing."

But Lacy didn't hear her over her own gasp. There, where the map had hung for as many years as she could recall, was a collage of photographs. Selfies, every one of them. Of her.

Bella stepped forward, scrutinizing the collection in silence.

Wren spoke up. "Now I remember! Your mother placed all those pictures there, Lacy. For safekeeping."

Lacy turned to Wren. "Safekeeping?"

"Your mother became a little eccentric in her later years." Wren offered a good-natured smile, as if what she was saying was the most natural thing in the world. She chuckled. "Your poor father. He couldn't always understand why she wanted to do certain things, but I know that she did them out of love. Like putting those pictures up there where they didn't get lost and she would always know where to find them."

"If she remembered," Bella said.

"Oh, I think she knew they were there somehow."

Lacy examined the wall, all the photos that she had taken long before iPhones could be found in homes all over the world. It was much more difficult to take a selfie back then, a challenge that had been part of the draw for Lacy. It was also the reason so many of them showed only part of her face, such as her eyes, her summertime freckles, and there was even one of her face split down the center, one eye peering mysteriously into the camera.

Her eyes welled. She blinked rapidly, her long-held belief that she had always been the invisible one disintegrating faster than she could try to prop it back up.

"You know," Wren said, "I think your mom once told me she thought you might become a famous photographer someday."

Lacy inhaled and smiled. "Yeah?"

"Mm-hm. She was quite proud of you and, if I recall correctly, a little wistful too. She prayed often for you. I remember she and I sitting here, looking at those pictures and her saying, 'My Lacy is growing up too fast!'" She sighed. "There are a lot of memories that your mother left with me."

For the next hour, Wren regaled Lacy and Bella with stories of their mother, many they had heard before and some new, such as how much she enjoyed sushi until she was pregnant with Bella and could no longer stand the smell of it, and how she would sneak over to the Mcafee home late at night to sneak a glass of wine with Wren while their families slept.

"Momma sounds just like you," Bella quipped to Lacy.

"Your Mom was a little like all of you," Wren said.

It was all too much for Lacy and she felt pretty, well, silly right now. Though it was difficult to pull her gaze away from her mother's careful placement of all her photographs, Lacy turned quickly. She bent down and wrapped her arms around Wren and hugged her.

"Thank you so much for sharing your memories with me." She sniffled through a smile. "It means more to me than you will ever know—and has explained so much."

FINN HAD BEEN in Las Vegas for more than a week and the place had never seemed so ... dull. The lights dreary. The shows uninteresting. The only thing that had helped him from going mad was the constant work. Adrian had been in the hospital longer than anyone had expected. As it turned out, he was not as forthcoming about his medical issues as Finn had hoped.

Thankfully, though, he was about to be released into the comfort of his own golf course-view home.

For now, Finn would continue to kneel down in the weeds of work. He had stayed in the sales and marketing offices until late each night, meeting with staff and digging through files of upcoming events that would be held at the resort. The catering and sales teams had stepped up, taking on additional clients, and he himself had familiarized himself with every detail.

What had surprised him most was Lacy's touch on nearly every file. After picking up the tenth file containing her notes, he put in a call to Adrian's executive assistant.

"Am I missing something here, Drew?" he said. "Or is Ms. Holloway involved in every large event slated for this year?"

"I believe she is, sir."

"I'd like you to pull Ms. Holloway's employment records and give me an accounting of the number of hours she has put in since January."

"Yes, sir."

Finn hung up, still questioning how Lacy could manage to be so intricately involved with back-to-back upcoming events. His stomach sank. She had obviously worked non-stop, despite the lack of a promotion. He wondered how she felt, if perhaps she suspected she had been lured to the company under false pretenses.

She should have been the one here handling things in Adrian's absence—not him. Though his staff was quite capable of picking up the files and running with the details, Lacy had the intimate knowledge to make each event shine. He was sure of it.

Finn had never intended for her to feel bypassed, ignored. And yet ... had his motives been entirely pure? Had he unintentionally hoped that Lacy's presence would nudge his brother into early retirement but never explicitly promise her this would happen?

A heavy sigh escaped him. He shoved the file cabinet drawer shut, sending dust flying. On one hand, spending this much time touching base with clients and details had helped his quest to dull the pain of rehashing all that had occurred between him and Lacy in Colibri Beach.

On the other hand, he now second-guessed himself about ... all of it. His mouth twisted as he stood awkwardly in the file room, considering the last few weeks. He could have handled things better, could have been upfront with Lacy about his thoughts, but would she have trusted him anyway?

He had been rash. Moved too fast. It was unlike Finn to

move forward on a project so quickly, to gut react when he spotted a potential property. He usually preferred to sit back and allow vultures to squabble over a prime piece, then swoop in when they had all but cannibalized each other.

Maybe that's what he thought he had been doing with Paige, too. If he were truthful, he had to admit he had been rather blasé about their relationship. At least in the beginning. He enjoyed the heads turning when they walked into a restaurant together, the flurry of attention nights out with her had brought him. But he had been in no hurry for marriage mainly because—and this was difficult to admit— he never believed he had too much to lose.

Unlike now. Now, it was as if his entire future balanced so precariously on the edge that one small misstep could send him into the abyss.

By Sunday, Lacy had stripped the walls of anything that felt personal to the house. Everything, that is, except the beloved map. After she had removed the myriad photographs and safely tucked them away in her belongings, she wiped down the map, had it framed at a shop to the south of Colibri, and with Bella's help, hung it back on the wall.

Bella stuck around for the weekly call, saying it was the least she could do after Seabiscuit had shed all over the place and caused all kinds of ruckus in the form of chewed-up sandals and a thong-on-his-head incident during Lacy's final week at the house. Bella had plans to do some wandering up the coast for a few days before taking her turn in the house for a month, but figured she could wait another day before leaving.

Lacy didn't mind the company at all. She welcomed it, actually. She had turned a corner, so to speak, where her family was concerned, no longer blaming them for bygones so stridently.

"I don't think we need much catching up, Lacy," Grace said when they were all on the call. "The walls looked fairly sparse when we were there the other day and, in some respects, it didn't look as much like our house anymore."

Bella frowned. "It's sad."

Grace half-frowned into the camera. "I didn't mean it that way. What I meant is that it will be much easier to sell the house if it doesn't feel like home to us, at least not the home we once knew."

"If that's the direction we ultimately decide to go," Jake said.

Maggie nodded, her expression introspective.

Lacy was spent. She didn't feel as if she had all that much to add at the moment and found herself sinking deeper into the couch that she had, ultimately, decided not to replace.

She couldn't seem to bear it.

"I can't believe Mom hid all those photos behind that map," Grace said, pulling Lacy into the conversation.

"I can." Maggie, already back from her brief honeymoon, looked tan and relaxed through the screen. "Lacy, you were so shy about those pictures. Don't you remember?"

Lacy shrank back. "Me?"

Jake cut in, "Yeah, her? Shy?"

"Yes, you were. One time I remember you telling Mom to burn those photos. And for all I knew, she had done it."

Bella gasped. "That would have been a tragedy!"

"It's okay that you don't remember." Maggie had opted to don satiny pajamas and call in from the comfort of her new home several blocks away. She fluffed her pillow and sat back. "It's a symptom of growing old."

"Speak for yourself." Lacy took a sip of wine and adjusted a pillow behind her own back, which had been twinging all day. She wanted to avoid a repeat of the day Finn had found her sprawled on the floor. Well, a repeat of the pain she felt radiating through her back—not of seeing him. She missed him more than she ever imagined she would.

Jake said, "I would just like to point out, ladies, that I am still quite young and virile."

"Oh gag!" Maggie laughed.

He chuckled. Bella giggled. And Grace huffed out a few belly laughs.

Lacy's mind, however, tumbled back to the other day, when Wren sat with her and Bella at the family's old dining table. The only thing she remembered right now is how much she had, over time, forgotten.

"Something on your mind, Lacy?" Grace, who seemed to have taken the lead tonight, zeroed in on her.

"I was just thinking about some of the things Wren told us the other day and I"—she licked her lips, thinking, then placed her glass of wine on the coffee table—"I think I owe you all an apology."

Grace frowned. "Really? What did you do to us?"

"I've been hard on you all—not that you're perfect or anything."

"Nice apology!" Jake cut in.

Lacy waved him away. "Seriously, I have always felt somewhat—I don't know—invisible in this family. You all have to admit there are far more pictures of all of you than of, well, of me." She shook her head. "Then I realized, I wasn't really angry at all of you, but inexplicably at our sweet mother."

Bella wore a sad pout.

"I have to hand it to Wren, though. The old bird set me straight."

"Careful. That's my future mother-in-law you are referring to."

Lacy playfully stuck her tongue out at her brother, then wiped away an errant tear with the back of her hand.

"Oh, honey," Maggie said, "that's grief."

"I agree with that one hundred percent," Grace added.

Even Jake nodded solemnly.

Lacy hauled in a full and lingering breath. "Well," she said, carefully, "seeing everyone together at Maggie's wedding gave me renewed hope. It gave me faith that"—she shrugged —"maybe we aren't all a bunch of knuckleheads after all."

"Oh, swoon!" Grace said, gentle laughter in her voice. "Do you use those same kinds of sweet nothings on Finn?"

Lacy swallowed and flickered her glance away from the screen toward Bella, who gave her an appropriately stricken look.

Maggie's voice broke through the thick silence, her question posed softly. "What is happening with Finn, Lacy?"

She returned her gaze to the group. "While there are some things that I have learned to hold onto this past few weeks, my future with Finn isn't one of them."

"I'm so sorry to hear that," Grace said. "But I think he'll

come around—even Chase commented on what a good match you two were."

"Yeah, I really like that guy for you," Mags added.

"Want me to rough him up?" Jake asked.

Lacy cast her brother a blithe look, one that neither accepted his offer nor completely shut it down.

"No matter what happens, we're here for you, kiddo." Grace gave Lacy a pointed, unwavering gaze.

"Here, here!" Maggie added.

Bella leaned over and looped an arm around Lacy's neck. "It's true! We got you." Bella's dog climbed into Lacy's lap. "See? Even Seabiscuit agrees."

Lacy's eyes flitted from person to person. "Got it. You're all here for me. Check."

"Now don't get all sassy on us," Maggie said. "Or else I might have to come over there in my jammies and join you and Bella for a group hug."

Lacy collapsed back onto the couch. "Give! I'm okay, you guys. Really, really!" *Liar, liar.*

"You'll be all right, Lacy. Promise," Grace said.

"You're right. I will." Lacy pulled herself off of the couch. Her heart might be twisting in confusion right now, but she had gained so much these past few months, how could she allow a little thing like heartbreak to shatter her? She couldn't. She wouldn't. "Are we done? Because I've got a project calling my name upstairs."

One by one they each said good night, except for Bella who wistfully whispered, "Until next time."

After the screen went black, Lacy washed and rinsed her wineglass and set it on a mat to dry.

Bella followed after her. "Want me to help you with your project?"

"No, thank you." Lacy stopped before heading down the hall. "I think I'm going to go for a walk on the beach first."

"At night? All by yourself?"

Lacy gave Bella a sad little smile. "Don't wait up."

10

"Thank you, Lillian."

Finn ended his call with the dragon lady of Colibri Beach, the smile of his heart leading the way. Thousand-thread-count sheets hadn't cured his insomnia. After spending the past week tossing around sleeplessly each night, he'd finally received the call he had been waiting for. And this time, his quick thinking did not give him pause.

With his pilot at the ready, Finn boarded a flight to California bringing a packed bag and a loaded question with him. He only hoped that Lacy Holloway was as ready for him as he was for her.

After landing, he eschewed his need for a driver and instead rented a Tesla for the ride. He would have plenty of charge to make it to Colibri in one try.

In his haste, it had not occurred to him how late he would arrive. Chalk that up to another change from his usual plotting and planning ways. He pulled into the driveway of the vacation rental, glad he had not yet officially vacated the place. Oh, he had left with no plans to return, but perhaps it had been serendipitous that he had neglected to tell anyone about that.

Quickly, he put his bags inside and flung open the back door to let the sea air in. He wanted to speak to Lacy now, but he'd have to wait. He stretched slightly and allowed his gaze to fall on the Holloway home. For all he knew, she still had a full house over there and what he wanted to say was meant only for her ears—and heart.

He stewed. And paced. And ultimately wound up leaning onto the railing of the back deck. He wished that he could blink and watch the sun rise, ushering in a new day. Instead, with night fully upon him, Finn grunted and pushed off the railing.

He was just about to go inside for the night when he spotted a flash of something. He narrowed his eyes, focusing. Someone was walking away from the shoreline toward him, her gait slow and uneven, yet achingly familiar.

Lacy.

Finn sucked in a breath. Without further sound, he kicked his shoes off the deck and descended the stairs two at a time. He jogged toward her, his feet landing deeply in the sand, his heartbeat quick and erratic.

She said nothing when he reached her, but let her eyes traverse his face, her gaze washing over him like a million fluttering wings. He reached for her and she ... winced.

He dipped his chin. "Are you all right?"

She tried to smile. Her hand went to her side and he noticed then the limp when she shifted from one leg to the other.

"Are you hurt?"

She flashed him a pained look. "What are you doing here?"

He slipped his hand around her waist. "You're hurt."

"Back was twinging tonight and it's gotten progressively worse with each step." She took another step, favoring her right side, so he tightened his hold on her.

"Slow down, Lacy. Let me help you."

"I'm fine."

"You are not fine."

"Did you come all the way from, from … wherever you went just to berate me?"

He chuckled. "If that's what it takes for you to slow down, then yes. I did."

Lacy groaned. She trembled lightly.

"That's it. Put your arm around my neck." Finn gently scooped Lacy up, despite her protests. "Unless I'm hurting you, you are wasting your breath."

"I can walk on my own."

"You can limp on your own." He trudged forward with Lacy in his arms, careful not to jostle her too much.

Lacy exhaled a groan. "You disappeared without saying goodbye."

"That all you got?" Finn responded. "Because if I remember correctly, you said you didn't want to see me anymore." He didn't add that she quit her job—wouldn't want her to misconstrue his actions as business related. They were far from it.

She stiffened in his arms when they reached his back deck. "Put me down."

"Only if you promise not to run."

"Seriously, Finn, what has gotten into you? I'm not a dog."

He lifted his brows, flirtatious. "I should say not."

She smiled, in spite of herself, he thought, and looked away. He wasn't fooled. Or at least, he hoped he wasn't.

Lacy returned his gaze, her eyes glistening, her mouth shaped into a definite pout. Gently, he put her down and helped her to stand.

"Lean on me," he said.

She shook her head. "I can't."

Finn swallowed the smile that had been burgeoning on his face since the moment he realized it was Lacy walking out there on the beach. He stepped back, considering her.

"Lacy."

"Finn."

They spoke each other's name at the same time.

"You go," he said.

Lacy wrapped her arms around herself, shivering. "I think we should talk."

He nodded. "You're cold. Let's go inside." When she didn't respond right away, he opened the door for her and added, "I promise to keep my hands to myself."

Wordlessly, she led the way inside his vacation rental. He followed her into the expansive living room and watched as she gingerly sat down, bracing an arm on the overstuffed end of the leather loveseat. Seeing her in pain made his stomach drop.

"Wine?" He asked this, hoping he had left some behind.

"No. Thank you."

"Water?"

She glared at him. "Are you going to sit down or not?"

"Yes, ma'am." He pulled up an ottoman and sat down in front of her, their knees brushing against each other.

"I have something I want … I want to say to you."

He reached for her hands, pleased that she did not resist. He cupped her hands in his. "I have something to tell you as well."

Lacy sat up, winced, and let herself flop back against the loveseat. "Me first, okay?"

"Of course."

"I've had a lot to think about the past few days, and I'm … embarrassed." She sighed. "I've already apologized to my siblings and now I want to apologize to you."

"You don't owe me that."

"Shush."

He shut his mouth and nursed a smile directed at her.

"I remembered something that you said to me … when you saw that selfie I took years ago. You said it looked like a story ready to be told. Finn, that—that meant a lot to me. A lot. It was as if you"—she looked into his eyes—"really saw me. Or at least wanted to."

Finn squeezed Lacy's hands. "I want to know everything about you."

She sucked in a breath, her brows knitting together. He wondered if she believed him so he leaned forward until their mouths were mere inches apart. "I guess I lied."

"About?"

"About keeping my hands off of you." Her lovely lips curved into a smile and he couldn't help himself. Finn leaned in and kissed her, sparks igniting in his head. His eyes snapped back open and he whispered, "Ah, Lacy."

A single tear dripped down her cheek. "I am sorry, Finn.

Sorry for misjudging you. I believe you really do see me. I've been horrible. Angry at my parents for ignoring me, even though they didn't. Not really. I've been dealing with my own hurts, my own grief." She huffed out a big, fat sigh. "I know that now."

Finn's heart careened against the wall of his chest. Instinctively, he touched her face with one hand, and then the other. He wanted her to know—needed her to know—how much she meant to him. "I have been a stupid man, Lacy. Slow to act sometimes, even slower to see. I have watched you from afar for some time, but threw obstacles of my own making into our way."

"I haven't been much help, though, have I?"

His smile turned rueful. "On the contrary, I'm glad you gave me my comeuppance. I needed to know that I hurt you because, well, that's not something I ever meant to do. Or ever want to do again." He hung his head a moment before looking back to her. "I have my own trust issues, you know."

"Paige?"

Finn sighed. "I hadn't realized just how cynical that experience made me at times, not quick to trust. I knew I was falling for you, but when you resisted me last week, I froze. I began to question my judgment and found myself pulling away from you. I went to Las Vegas to check on Adrian, but in reality, I was nursing my own inability to trust in a relationship again. I realize now how tragic that kind of thinking is."

Lacy gently pulled his hands away and leaned forward, no sign of the back pain that had pinned her down earlier. She brushed his cheek with a touch of her hand. "I'm sorry for the hurt you experienced. That must have been heartbreaking for you and I want you to know that I trust you, Finn. I"—she paused, tears filling her eyes. "I love you."

He sucked in a breath, his gaze traveling over her beauty, her unabashed declaration of love careening through him, messing with his ability to see straight. "Missing out on you would have been the biggest tragedy of all. I love you wholly and completely, Lacy."

She was crying now, full and heavy tears that flooded her face. "There's more, Finn. I've been thinking about the last time I saw you. I was childish. That old house isn't mine to give, and if it were going to be sold, I would want it to go to you."

Finn began to wag his chin. He didn't want to talk about anything other than the two of them right now.

But she continued, her eyes shiny and loving. Her caress rich. "If you believe that the ghost house is the perfect place for Hastings Resorts to make its mark on the coast, then I support you. I fully do."

LACY HARDLY SLEPT ALL NIGHT, but this time it had nothing to do with heartbreak—and everything to do with anticipation. She and Finn had talked for hours, until she could hardly keep her eyes open and nearly curled up on his couch to fall asleep. But he'd rousted her. Said he was concerned about her back—rightly so—and carried her home.

She'd protested about that, the carrying home part, but what can a woman do when a handsome man wants to display all-out chivalry? Once inside, they laughed all the way through the house, admonishing each other to keep it down when they passed the whale-themed room where Bella slept. Carefully, Finn lowered her to the bed in the upstairs master bedroom, his expression turning sober.

"You're killing me here, you know." There was a growl to his voice that she hadn't experienced before. He kissed her tenderly, the passion of it lingering on her lips.

"Shoo," she whispered. "Before I—"

He centered a challenge on her, a fierceness in his expression.

She swallowed back a reply, staggered by the desire displayed in his eyes. She steadied herself with one long breath and said, "Before we wake up my baby sister."

Finn chuckled. He kissed her on the forehead, followed by one on her nose, then looked her squarely in the eyes. "Good night, beautiful." She listened as he stepped softly down the stairs and out of the house.

Now as she waited for Finn to pick her up this morning, she relived the night before that had changed everything for them. There were questions still, such as how they would make a long-distance relationship work and what type of career she would pursue. After realizing how much Adrian wanted her out of the Vegas resort, she was adamant about never returning, but she wasn't sure if she was meant for the hotel business anymore anyway.

"You've got a dumb look on your face." Bella stood in the living room, Seabiscuit in one arm and a paper bag stuffed with clothes in the other. She tilted her head to one side, a touch of sarcasm in her smile.

"Unlike the bag lady moment you're having right now."

Bella glanced at the bag. "This? Just a few things to take with me on my quick getaway. I didn't want to take my whole suitcase."

Lacy rolled her eyes. She stood to her feet and marched down the hall to the bedroom. Seconds later she emerged with a small, black overnight bag. "Here." She plunked it down on the floor beside Bella. "Use this so I'm not ashamed for you to represent the fam."

Bella frowned, though it looked fake. "You were nicer last night. Did something happen to bring the old Lacy back?"

A knock on the door interrupted Lacy's retort. She nearly flew toward it. When Finn entered, he immediately kissed her, a sizzling kiss that sent her nerve endings into a tizzy.

"So I guess I have my answer," Bella quipped.

"Hey, Bella." Finn tipped a nod to her.

"Hey yourself, Finn. Good to see you back."

A smile lit his face. "Not as good as it is to be here." He turned to Lacy and offered her his arm. "Ready to go?"

She took his arm and turned to Bella, who shook her head.

"I got it," Bella said with a laugh. "Don't wait up."

Lacy scowled good-naturedly. "I was going to say have a nice trip."

"Okay, you're being nice again. You win." Bella laughed. "I'll lock up after I repack."

When Lacy slid into Finn's rental car, the aroma of roast chicken greeted her. She hadn't asked him where they were going, but she didn't care either. They were together again, and at the moment, that's all that mattered to her. It didn't hurt either that the sun was out and the day gorgeous. Had the sky always been this clear? This blue?

He drove north, and as he approached a familiar area of town, her heart squeezed. The ghost house. She had said last night that she would support the old place becoming a resort, but did she have to be reminded of that right now?

Lacy cast a glance at Finn who seemed unflustered by her sudden silence. Her heart fluttered at the sight of him. The swath of scruff on his skin, the telling dimple in his cheek, the lines at the corners of his eyes that grew longer with his smile.

He turned up the steep driveway and suddenly she didn't care at all about the transformation that would take place. Things were different now. She had run to this place as a kid, still growing into who she would someday be. She still was, but she sensed a renewal in herself that couldn't be achieved overnight.

They reached the top of the hill and she smiled at the old house. She saw the saggy porch anew, the outer walls that needed paint, and she realized that greater things lay ahead —for both her and that property.

He parked at the edge of the lot and opened her door. "Thought we would have a picnic up here."

"Mm. The reason your car smelled so good."

He kissed her on the cheek and grinned. "And here I thought you were appreciating my cologne."

She raised a brow. "Poulet by Dior?"

"Oui." Finn flashed her another grin. "I didn't realize you spoke French."

"I only know the French word for chicken." She clucked twice.

"Learning more and more about you as the days go on, my dear." He lifted his chin, laughing.

"Just you wait."

He was still chuckling as they walked to the rim of the land together. He wore a backpack and held a basket and blanket. They stopped beneath the branches of her favorite tree and he handed her the picnic basket. She held onto it while he fanned the blanket out on a flat area of earth. As she curled up on the blanket, leaning on her arm and hip, he fished a fat pillow out of the backpack.

"Here," he said, propping it behind her arm. "If you need to lean on something, it's yours."

"You really do think of everything."

"That remains to be seen." He rolled onto his behind and bent one knee toward the sky, leaning his arm across it.

She watched as his expression went from jovial to pensive the longer he looked out toward the West. Gently, she pushed forward and slipped her arms about his waist, clasping her hands in front of his middle. Lacy rested her temple on Finn's shoulder, her body melting into his, the rhythm of their breaths syncing.

She could have stayed there, in that position, all day.

He threaded his fingers through one of her hands and turned to her, causing her other arm to slide around to his back.

"Lacy," he whispered, his mouth against her hair.

She felt herself sinking, immersed in him, startled by it all and yet completely at ease with him. He kissed her and she allowed herself to feel every bit of it, the softness, the intensity—the adoration.

They parted and he held her face between his hands,

tipping his forehead toward hers. His breathing was labored, and after a few seconds, he huffed out a grin. "I have so much to tell you, but you are distracting me."

"I'm not doing anything."

"Oh," he said pointedly, "you're doing something."

She laughed, pulling away from him. "Start talking then, I won't interrupt. I promise."

He tightened his jaw and dipped a rather doubtful look at her. "But will I be able to resist you? That's the question." He bit down on his bottom lip for a moment. "Hear me out."

"Of course."

"I need your help."

"Anything."

"You haven't heard what I'm about to ask."

"As long as it doesn't involve sushi I'm pretty sure you won't have any pushback."

"Fine. I want you to help me train Adrian's replacement at the hotel."

She waited. This was what he wanted to ask her?

"And I'd like you to help me scout more properties for Hastings Resorts."

Heat rose in Lacy's cheeks. She said she'd do anything for him. Well, anything but eat raw fish. But work? He was asking her to go back to work for him? After all they'd been through?

"I don't know what to say, Finn."

"Say yes."

"I-I already said that I wasn't interested in going back to the resort, and I love the idea of traveling with you"—she snapped a look out to the horizon, wondering how far to take this. She exhaled—"but I have to figure out where my life is headed, what my future looks like."

Finn rolled onto his knees. "Perfect."

"What do you mean? Why is that perfect? I thought we came up here to be together, not talk about—" She gasped.

Finn was still on his knees, smiling at her, but somewhere in the middle of her angsty reply to him, he had produced a diamond in the palm of his hand. He lifted the dazzling ring by his fingers and held it out to her.

"I'm not asking you to be my employee, Lacy Holloway, but my wife. I adore you—I think I knew that minutes after we first met more than a year ago, though I was too dense to realize. I don't want to live one more second of this life without you by my side. Will you marry me?"

For the first time that she could ever remember, Lacy was without words. Fresh emotion pressed through her, her mind taking in Finn Hastings kneeling on a blanket with a gorgeous rock in his hand, asking her to marry him.

She reached for his hand, her fingers drifting over the ring, and the tears began to fall.

He tipped her chin up and kissed her sweetly, then asked her again. "Marry me?"

"Yes. I will absolutely, truly, one hundred percent marry you!" She kissed him back.

"Okay, but only if you're sure."

She laughed now, overwhelmed by him. Finn slipped the engagement ring onto her finger and kissed her hand. Then he reached for a knife, leaned over to the tree, and found the spot where she had carved her initials so long ago.

She gasped as he carved his alongside hers.

"There," he said. "Now it's complete. Don't you think?"

"It's ... perfect."

"C'mon," he said. "Let's get a picture."

Finn pulled her along toward the old house and together they climbed the rickety steps to the porch. She sucked in a breath. While she had been brazen enough to sneak onto the property often, it had been years since she had dared to actually step onto this porch. The view was nothing short of wondrous and for a split second she regretted their coming here. Not because she didn't want to be with Finn, but she simply didn't want to sully the joy of this day with any regret over the property being redeveloped.

Finn lifted his phone as far as his arms would reach. "Hold up your ring finger and I'll take a shot of us smooching."

Lacy laughed lightly. "Don't you want to turn around so that the view is behind us?"

"No, this is perfect. One ... two ... three." She held up her hand for the camera to see as he kissed her on the cheek, the goofiest look on his face.

They sat on the porch awhile, listening to the wind tangle in the trees, Finn's strong arm curled around her. She loved everything about this moment: the sound, the sense of belonging—him. Where she and Finn would go next, she didn't know. She didn't care either. As long as they were together.

Lacy's stomach growled and Finn laughed. He stood and offered her his hand, pulling her up until she stood in his embrace. "I need to feed you, apparently."

"Or I could just live on love."

"I have so much of it to give, Lacy. I'm going to spend the rest of my life showing you just how much." Finn leaned down and kissed her again until the heat of it curled her hair. "Let's take one more photo before we go, shall we?"

He raised the phone, took the shot, and showed her the screen. "I thought it would be nice to have a few pictures of the place before the demolition."

Lacy's smile dimmed. "Of course."

He raised a brow. "You do want to remodel the place, right? Add some rooms? Brighten up the exterior?"

She bit her lip, looking from him to the house and back again. "I'm confused. Are you leaving the house and building around it? Or did you decide on going forward with my idea of turning this into a boutique property with fewer rooms but more amenities?"

He touched her face, his eyes zeroed in on her, unwavering. "Lacy, I bought the ghost house for you. For us."

She stared at him, a pinprick of light beginning to dawn.

He pulled her closer, the warmth of him all-encompassing, his gaze endearing. "I can't promise how often we will be here—that's something for us to discuss together—but I saw the way you loved this place the first time you brought me up here. And I knew I wanted you both."

With a fresh tear trailing down her cheek, Lacy lifted her chin, wanting him to kiss her and knowing he would. She loved him. Plain. Simple. More than that, Finn had revealed a glimpse into his own heartbreak, and overnight she had grown protective of him. He was everything she had dared to hope for, and then some, and with him, she felt the ghosts of her past—fear, doubt, invisibility—flitting away.

"I'm overwhelmed. Stunned," she said. "You didn't have to do this!"

"For the beautiful brunette with the bad back and a penchant for good wine? Oh yes," he said. "Yes, I did."

Then Finn kissed her again as the old house looked on, patiently waiting for new life to fill its long-empty halls so it could stand as a testament to love, hope, and faith.

And Lacy couldn't wait to oblige.

ALSO BY JULIE CAROBINI

Julie's books are available wherever books are sold. Please visit Julie's website for details: JulieCarobini.com

Beach House Romances

Beach Sunrise (book 1)

Beach Memories (book 2)

Beach Secrets (book 3)

Beach Sunset (book 4)

Beach Music (book 5)

Standalone

Reunion in Saltwater Beach

Hollywood by the Sea Novels

Chasing Valentino (book 1)

Finding Stardust (book 2)

Sea Glass Inn Novels

Walking on Sea Glass (book 1)

Runaway Tide (book 2)

Windswept (book 3)

Beneath a Billion Stars (book 4)

A Sea Glass Christmas (book 5)

<u>**Otter Bay Novels**</u>

Sweet Waters (book 1)

A Shore Thing (book 2)

Fade to Blue (book 3)

The Otter Bay Novel Collection (books 1-3)

<u>**The Chocolate Series**</u>

Chocolate Beach (book 1)

Truffles by the Sea (book 2)

Mocha Sunrise (book 3)

<u>**Cottage Grove Cozy Mysteries**</u>

The Christmas Thief (book 1)

The Christmas Killer (book 2)

The Christmas Heist (book 3)

Cottage Grove Mysteries (books 1-3)

ABOUT THE AUTHOR

JULIE CAROBINI is the author of 22+ inspirational beach romances. Her books feature captivating heroines, endearing heroes, and a cast of quirky friends, all bound together by the secrets they keep. Her bestselling titles include *Walking on Sea Glass, Runaway Tide,* and *Reunion in Saltwater Beach.* Julie has received awards for writing and editing from The National League of American Pen Women and ACFW, and she is a double finalist for the ACFW Carol Award. She is the mother of three grown kids and lives on the California coast with her husband, Dan, and their rescue pup, Dancer.

Please visit her at
www.juliecarobini.com